Confessions of a Teenage Drag King

MARKUS HARWOOD-JONES

JAMES LORIMER & COMPANY LTD., PUBLISHERS
TORONTO

James Lorimer & Company Ltd., Publishers acknowledges funding support from the Ontario Arts Council (OAC), an agency of the Government of Ontario. We acknowledge the support of the Canada Council for the Arts, which last year invested $153 million to bring the arts to Canadians throughout the country. This project has been made possible in part by the Government of Canada and with the support of Ontario Creates.

Cover design: Gwen North
Cover image: Shutterstock

9781459415614
eBook also available 9781459415591
Cataloguing data for the hardcover edition is available from Library and Archives Canada.

Library and Archives Canada Cataloguing in Publication (Paperback)

Title: Confessions of a teenage drag king / Markus Harwood-Jones.
Names: Harwood-Jones, Markus, 1991- author.
Series: Real Love. Description: Series statement: Real love
Identifiers: Canadiana (print) 20200217674 | Canadiana (ebook) 20200217682 | ISBN 9781459415584 (softcover) | ISBN 9781459415591 (EPUB)
Classification: LCC PS8615.A775 C66 2020 | DDC jC813/.6—dc23

Published by:
James Lorimer &
Company Ltd., Publishers
117 Peter Street, Suite 304
Toronto, ON, Canada
M5V 0M3
www.lorimer.ca

Distributed in Canada by:
Formac Lorimer Books
5502 Atlantic Street
Halifax, NS, Canada
B3H 1G4

Distributed in the US by:
Lerner Publisher Services
1251 Washington Ave. N.
Minneapolis, MN, USA
55401
www.lernerbooks.com

Printed and bound in Canada.
Manufactured by Marquis in Toronto, Ontario in August 2020.
Job #355125

For my grandparents.

01 Blue Light

THE STAGE IS MY HOME. I live in the glare of the lights, the beat of the music. I bask among sweaty binders, slipping breast forms, drying glue on cheeks and brows. I wink into existence as I run a hand across my flattened chest. Lifted by the screams of the crowd, I hit my next turn.

I walk offstage. Tara Dactyl tosses me a bottle of water from the DJ booth. I shake off beads of sweat as I snatch it and swig. I flash a grin back toward the spotlight. Stormé Waters is already on stage. Riding the high I left in my wake, she starts hyping up the next act.

Earl Grey slips next to me. Their face is glowing from the phone that's practically glued to their nose.

I flick a couple droplets toward their pasted-on pointy ears. "Warmed 'em up for you."

Earl laughs and pats their wig in place before snapping a selfie. "Thanks Ren! I got some pics of you for Insta, mind returning the favour?"

"All right, gaybies!" Stormé calls from up front. "Give it up for our very own hot, hot Earl Grey!"

"That's my cue!" says Earl with one last nervous smile. Climbing on stage, they nearly slip on a wet patch by the stairs. I wince, then spin on my heel back toward the bar.

I flag down the bartender, Joni, for my regular — a screwdriver, virgin of course. The Barn keeps it dry on Sundays, at least before ten. You'd never guess it though. Guess a good drag show gets the crowd going, booze or no.

Pulling out my phone, I go to record Earl's latest take at the sexy *Star Trek* thing. I have to admit, they know how to work their weird, dorky style. First time I ever saw Earl on stage, it was like I'd slipped into a whole different world. Even now, after they've taught me their tricks, they've still got that special something. It's not until their set's almost done that I look down and realize I forgot to press record.

"Hey, pal," Joni says and slides over my drink. I go for my wallet but she holds up a manicured hand. "It's taken care of." Across the bar, a giggling trio watches me. I shoot my fans a wink as I take my first sip. Just another perk of being a king.

I'm about to go greet my admirers when I feel a buzzing at my wrist. My parents, again. Dismissing the call on my smartwatch, I wave at Joni. "Tell the others I said bye." She raises an eyebrow but gets caught up taking more orders. On stage, Stormé closes out the night.

My breath is fog in the cool air of Church Street. Blue lights burn from the neon signs of the strip.

Wiggling my fingers, I let the heat of the bar fade. I pass under clouds of vape smoke rising from people on stoops outside crowded pubs. A noisy couple grinds in an alley, while tourists try to take night-time selfies at the rainbow crosswalk.

Cold bites at my lungs. The transit app says I've got ten minutes until the next streetcar. I hunker down in the bus shelter, squeezing my pink fists. Maybe I should have brought gloves.

A silhouette moves into view. The streetlight's glow filters through her hair like a halo. The bus stop's buzzing ad splashes blue across her round, wire-frame glasses. Her cheeks shimmer golden-brown.

I stand up quickly, slip on a patch of ice, and smack my funny bone against the shelter's metal frame. Biting back the awful tingling in my elbow, I flash what I hope is a dashing smile. "You at the Barn tonight?"

Sharp eyes take me in from behind a pair of round glasses.

"No."

"Too bad." I shrug. "Was one hell of a show."

"Anyone good?" She asks, her voice softer than I expected.

"Me, obviously!" I start to laugh but the cold hits my throat and turns it into a cough. "I'm Ren," I choke out.

A hint of a smile moves across the shadow of her face. "Clover."

"Clover." Her name warms my lips. "So where were you, then? I didn't think there were any other all-ages spots around here on Sunday nights."

"Who says I'm underage?" She looks out toward the empty streetcar tracks.

"My bad." I shrug again. "Maybe you've just got a baby face . . . or a fake ID."

Clover sighs mist into the night. "I just like to walk around sometimes."

"Cool, cool, cool." I loudly clear my throat. "So did you wanna, like, go grab a slice of pizza or . . ."

"Streetcar," she nods.

I look up and see an open streetcar door. I didn't even hear it pull up.

Cold slush edges in from the corners of my boots. I step in and tap my card. Clover stays put.

"You're not coming?" I ask.

"I'll catch the next one," she says.

The doors shut with a loud clack. I watch Clover slide from view as the driver grumbles something about moving away from the door.

I surf the rattle of the streetcar all the way to the very back. It's thankfully quiet. There are only a few other passengers, and all look too busy with their phones to notice one stray drag king. Sitting down, I spin my jacket and wear it like a blanket. I pinch loose the buttons of my shirt and slide my arms up my sleeves. I pull at the Velcro of my binding vest and tuck it into my coat pocket.

Next, I use a pre-packaged towelette to wipe the stubble off my cheeks. Then, a thin comb to coax my hair back down into floppy bangs that hide my face. Checking my reflection in the window, I peel off a stray fleck of spirit gum. Just in time. Above, flashing letters announce my stop.

I step off with a sigh, releasing the last of the person I was. I brush off any glitter still clinging to my jacket and pat myself down. In my pocket, I find my headphones. They flash red from the low battery. I walk home hearing only the soft crunch of my boots in the thin layer of snow.

The living room lights flick on as I come up the porch steps. Try as I might, the screen door creaks when I pull it open. In a second, there are two shadows waiting for me on the other side.

"We were so worried!" Mom coos. She pulls me into a hug before I can even get my keys out of the door. "Why didn't you answer our calls?"

"Sorry," I mumble, pulling back. I let my hair fall over my eyes. "Didn't see them."

"Why'd we spend all that money on that fancy what-cha-ma-thing, then?" Nathan asks, waving at my smartwatch with a forced scowl. He's terrible at playing the scary stepdad.

"Youth group went late." The familiar fib comes out warm and easy. "We went out for food after, so . . ."

Kicking aside my boots, I push past both of them and head upstairs.

"Wait one second, young lady," says Nathan. I glance back, daring him to follow through. ". . . Does that mean you don't need dinner?"

Mom pokes Nathan with her elbow. "Lauren?" she calls after me. I've got one hand already on the handle of my bedroom door. "Ready for tomorrow, kiddo?"

I grunt something that could be a yes and I disappear into my room. As I hop into bed, my wrist starts buzzing again. I'm suddenly flooded with notifications. Earl put up the pictures from tonight. There's a bunch of action shots of me on stage, all tagged @The.Real.Ren. The blue light of my phone burns into my eyes as I examine each image, fighting off sleep for a just little while longer.

02 Distraction

BEEP — BEEP — BEEP!

"Ugh," I grumble and smack my hand against the bed. Feeling through the mess of pillows and blankets, I pry my eyes open and lurch over. I snag my phone with my fingertips and drag it back like a claw-machine prize. I dismiss the alarm to try to get just a few seconds more sleep.

There's a knock at the door. "Lauri, you awake yet?" Mom asks, jiggling the handle. Maybe if I'm quiet long enough she'll leave me alone. Or she'll freak out, think I'm dead and try to break down the door. "Come down in five if you want Nathan to give you a ride!"

Letting out a groan, I force myself awake. I fall into some pants on the floor and nab a hoodie off the back of my chair. I take one last quick look in the mirror and tell myself, "Just a few more months of this bullshit." Pulling down my bangs, I'm ready as I'll ever be. It's the first day of my last semester of high school. I'm already so over it.

My school's not exactly big, but not that small either. It's downtown, but on a quiet street. We don't have a stellar sports team, or a hardcore debate club or any musicals to write home about. But we're not so bad that anyone really cares. I guess my school's a lot like me. No need to be the best, as long as you're not the bottom of the barrel.

Dodging bulging backpacks and hipsters with messenger bags, I keep my head down on my way to my locker. Bumping past a pack of slow walkers, I spot super-student Stephanie. Looks like she's talking to that bro-dude, Brian, again. That's a scandal that'll make its way around the school in no time. Brian puffs up his shoulders, trying to grab at Steph's phone while she giggles in protest. I shrug past them, wrinkling my nose.

Next to my locker, a paranoid-looking stoner is trying to Febreze his clothes. The stink mixes with waves of Axe body spray floating from the boys' washroom.

I try to focus on my locker combination. I think it's my mom's birthday. When is that again? I wish Nathan had just got me a proper lock like I asked for. Mom kept saying I'd lose the key. She's always stressing so much. Joke's on her. I just end up carrying my stuff all day instead of trying to get this impossible thing open.

"Prom committee?" my old buddy Rodger pushes through the hall, trying to pass out flyers. He spots me and smiles so wide I can see the rubber bands on his braces. "Lauri!"

"No thanks," I grumble. I try and fail again to open my locker.

"Come on," Rodger whines. His sweaty thumb is already streaking the ink on his pamphlet. "Just take one. For old time's sake?"

That's not going to work on me. Rodger and I go back to grade school, but that just means he of all people should know that I don't do extracurriculars. Still, I do kind of owe him one for helping me study for exams last term . . . every term, actually.

My fingers hover near the extended pamphlet. A giggle floats over my shoulder. Stephanie whispers something to Brian as she stares at the two of us. Rodger's smile falters as I pull back. I heft my bag on one shoulder. "Sorry," I mutter.

"This is like the Photography Collective all over again," he sighs, running a hand over his tight black curls.

The bell rings. "Not my problem," I tell him, and hurry off to first period.

Thanks to Rodger's pestering, I'm late for French and miss out on a window seat. I slump into a spot in the middle, keeping a good distance from the front-of-class splash zone. Not that it matters too much here.

I'm pretty sure Madame Dorit doesn't even really speak French. She seems happy enough to put on videos and wait out the clock with the rest of us.

My focus drifts as I let my pen move freely. I outline the stage, a figure standing in the spotlight. Me, I guess. The me that I am when I'm him. Ren. Swirling circles make up the faces of screaming fans. The platform shakes with clapping hands, stomping feet, heavy bass. As my eyes drift down, I notice a girl with round, wire-framed glasses looking back at me from the margins of the scene.

"Pass it back," says the kid in front of me. I snap out of my daydream as a handful of papers are heaped on my desk. Crappy word-searches and vague outlines for an essay due next week.

"Homework already?" I groan.

The bell rings and I practically jump out of my seat. "Pardonnez-moi," says Madame Dorit. "You're not dismissed until I —" Her protest is drowned out by backpacks zipping and damp sneakers slapping toward the door.

In second period gym we're supposed to be playing soccer-baseball, but Brian and Kyler get stuck arguing about who's taking Rodger on their team. Rod just sits there, like it isn't the most mortifying thing anyone could think of. Honestly, I'd feel more pity for him if he didn't bring it on himself so hard. He's always joining — or starting — every committee in existence. Last semester he even ran for student council!

Rodger's the kind of weirdo people notice, and not in a good way. Not like me. One of the perks to being the quiet kid is that people tend to forget if you're any good at anything. Which is better than everyone knowing for sure that you're straight up terrible.

"Hey, Lauri," says Morgan, pulling at her braid. She says hi to everybody, even invisibles like me. "I saw your pics! Fun weekend, eh?"

I freeze. My thoughts race. *How does she know about the show? Did she find Ren's Insta? Has she told anyone?!*

"Love a Nutella and Netflix binge!" Morgan laughs, elbowing me.

I melt back into reality. She means my other

account, @LaurenGarborator. I forget half the stuff I put on there. "Right, totally," I say. "Super fun. You do anything cool?"

"You didn't see already?" Morgan asks. She quickly checks if the teacher's watching and sneaks her phone out to pull up Facebook. "My moms got this new horse at the stables, and —"

She's cut off by a loud slam from the gym doors.

For a second, I think I must be dreaming. One of those dreams where you go through all the motions of the day and then wake up to find out you haven't even started yet. I blink a few times. But she's still standing there. At the far end of the gym, there's Clover. The heavy door swings back, slamming shut before she can stop it.

"Sorry," she apologizes to no one in particular. She pushes her glasses up her nose, speed walking towards the teacher.

"Have you met the new kid?" Morgan asks. I quickly drop my eyes, worried she's already caught me gawking. "I heard she got transferred here after flunking out of her last school."

"Yeah, no," Devon whispers behind us. "They kicked her out for smoking in the girls' room. That's why they make her get changed in the wheelchair bathroom."

"It's the *accessible* bathroom, dumbass," Sara chimes in. "And *I* heard she got her old school burned down!" I just roll my eyes. As if they'd send anybody that cool to this school.

"Clover Hines?" Ms. Dees, the gym teacher, taps anxiously on her clipboard. "You're late."

Clover mutters an apology. She pulls at her baggy gym clothes as she scans the room. I brace myself. If she recognizes me, I'll have to deny it. Deny everything. Everyone has a double, right? Plus, Ren doesn't even really look like me. Not with all that fake facial hair and contouring. And who's gonna believe the new kid anyway?

Thankfully, her eyes go right past me. I release my breath. Still invisible, for now.

03 *Feelings*

OPERATION: COUNTERING the Clover Crisis. The title barely fits at the top of my notebook page, but I've always thought good plans should have some alliteration in the name. After asking around, I've mostly figured out her schedule. Phys Ed. in the mornings, obviously. But Morgan told me during Math that Clover's other courses are the kind for university entry. So I should be safe, since I haven't taken a course at that level since grade ten.

"Garber?" Mr. Mandelo grumbles under his heavy moustache. "Garber?" I lazily flip my hand into the air. Mandelo gives a slight nod at my presence before moving on. "Hines?" he asks. I feel my entire body clench. This wasn't in the plan.

The door crashes open as Clover gasps into the room. "Here!"

"Welcome to College Biology, Ms. Hines," Mandelo grunts, checking her off his list.

"Uh, did you say college-level?" Clover looks around nervously. She's met with a wall of stares. "Sorry, maybe I made a mistake. I'm supposed to be —"

"You're on the attendance." Mandelo taps his clipboard. He peers over the tops of his bifocals. "Now, let's get you a seat."

"I'll take the new girl." Brian waves his hand from the back row. Stephanie slaps him hard on the shoulder, sending giggles through the rest of the class. Clover looks down, sheepishly pushing up her glasses.

"Garber," Mandelo huffs toward me. "You don't have a neighbour, do you?"

I glance at the clearly empty seat next to me. "...Yes?" I try.

"Good," he snorts through his moustache and goes back to the roll call.

Following instructions, Clover heads in my direction. I look down and realize my notebook is open. A drawing of her face stares up at me, alongside all the details of my top-secret operation! In a panic, I rip the page out and shove it into my mouth. I chomp down. Clover slowly sets down her binder next to me, wide-eyed. I smile, bits of paper bulging in my cheeks. *This is fine*, I tell myself. *I'm fine*. I just have to get through the next hour.

"Now, let's begin to prepare for the group assignment." Mandelo pushes himself up. The whole room groans as he loudly scrapes chalk across the board. I swear he pretends not to understand Smartboards just to mess with us. I wince at the awful sound, but what comes next is even worse. "The person sitting next to you right now is your partner."

Clover looks over at me with raised eyebrows. I swallow hard, choking on the mushy remnants of my failed plan.

"I can't get you two anything else?" asks the old woman. She looks a bit like a large raisin bringing us two cups of hot tea.

"No thanks, Granny," Clover says as she carefully takes the tray. "We really should just study."

"What about your friend?" Clover's grandmother arches her thin brows at me. "I'm sorry, I didn't catch your name, dear."

"It's Lauri," I say, eyeing Clover. She still hasn't said a word about meeting Ren the other night. Maybe if I keep going by my nickname, she won't put it together. "And, uh, I'm fine. Thanks, Mrs. Hines."

"You can call me Judy, dear," she says, patting her hands. She hovers by the door for a few seconds and smiles at the two of us. "You let me know if you need anything

". . . Clover." She winks like we're sharing a secret.

"Granny," Clover whines. "Can you just close the door, please?"

Mrs. Hines — Judy, I guess — purses her lips. She gives Clover a long look before closing the door two-thirds of the way. We're still in full view of the apartment's sitting room. Clover huffs but turns her focus back to our schoolwork.

"Do you have the outline?" she asks. I watch her flip through the colour-coded sections of her binder. "I think maybe Mr. Mandelo forgot to give me one . . ." My plan was to hang back, see if I could maybe swap partners with Morgan or something. But Clover insisted on meeting up right after school to start planning our Biology project. I can already tell this is going to be tough.

"It's cool you live with your grandma," I say, trying to keep it chill.

"It's okay," she mutters. She moves on to search through the chapters of her Bio textbook. "She goes to bed early, so I have to be quiet a lot of the time."

I go for my tea. It's burning hot and loaded with so much sugar it makes my teeth hurt. I sputter into my cup. Clover looks up at me, pursing her lips just like her grandma. "So, uh, just you and the old lady," I try to recover my cool, tongue still tingling. "Like something out of Spider-Man, or whatever."

Clover snorts, getting back to her search for the missing outline. "Except my parents aren't dead."

"They just booted you over here, eh?" I lean back on her springy single bed. "Figures. Parents suck."

My mind slips away. I start to daydream what music to pick for Ren's next routine. I can hardly wait until our next "youth group" Sunday. I'd hit up the Barn's stage to practise even sooner, but tiptoeing around Mom and Nathan is such a headache. If I ever told them where I was really going, I think Mom might have a literal heart attack.

Clover looks at me in desperation. "Are you sure you don't have it?"

I drop one hand down, digging through my backpack. I pull out a crumpled, somehow damp copy of the assignment guideline. Clover reaches out. When our fingers get close, a shock runs between us.

"Sorry!" she says quickly, pulling back.

"No, no, it's my — my bad," I pull back, shaking my hand. "Must've rubbed my socks on the carpet when I came in."

Clover just looks at me for a few seconds before breaking into a laugh. "You're so weird." She snatches the paper and tries to flatten it out against her textbook.

As Clover moves to adjust her glasses, I can't seem to look away. For some reason, I'm getting warm. Really warm. And I'm awfully aware of my breathing. My heart starts pounding in my chest. It almost feels like when I'm on stage, but all out of rhythm. Her lips look so soft and all I can think about is leaning over and . . .

"I've got to go!" I leap up, grabbing my bag.

"Already?" Clover gets up after me. "Granny doesn't go to bed until seven-thirty . . ."

"I just remembered my mom wants me home," I lie. I'm already giving a quick wave to Judy as I head toward the door.

Too antsy to wait for the elevator, I start down the stairs. On the second flight down, I slip and lose my footing. I catch the railing, gripping it tight and breathing heavily. What is wrong with me? Ren flirts with girls all the time . . . But that's different, isn't it? That's him. It's all just part of the act, the show.

This is real life. This is the real me! I don't catch feelings, especially not for anyone from school. I mean, there was that one time in grade nine when I asked Rodger to the Halloween dance. But that whole thing was so awkward, I don't think it counts.

My wrist vibrates. I figure it's Mom calling, checking when my study session is over. But it's Clover. She wants to know if we can meet up again tomorrow. My palms are so sweaty, I nearly slip down the stairs again. I tell myself I'll text her back later. After getting my footing.

04 Tempo

"FIVE-SIX, SEVEN-EIGHT," Stormé claps from the stage sidelines. Earl sits a few paces back, perched on the stairs leading up to the DJ booth. Their shiny new wig looks like it's about to slip off. Tara is starting sound check and blowing a large bubble of pink chewing gum. One of the speakers lets out a loud pop just as I hit my heel turn. "You're off, Ren," says Stormé, taking a sip from her massive water bottle.

I kick my feet against the hollow stage and step

out of my routine. "You're counting too fast," I tell her. "I know my song."

"You sure about that?" she asks. Before I can come up with a witty reply, Stormé's phone starts to chime. It's probably for the best that I got cut off. It's not smart to piss off your MC-slash-drag-mother right before a show.

Dismissing the alarm, Stormé fishes out a colourful pill caddy and pops a handful in her mouth. Estrobreak, I guess. Stormé's been on hormone replacement therapy for a few months now. She says the biggest change she's noticed is just the need for double the bathroom breaks during shows.

Stormé follows her dose with a swig of water. I wave my own empty bottle toward Earl and say, "Hey, you mind?"

"Sure, I was gonna check in with Joni anyway!" Earl scurries off, shedding glitter as they go. I chuckle. Earl might have taught me the ropes, but they're still the youngest of the group. And they can be a little . . . well, a lot. Tonight's outfit is no exception. While they may be taking a break from the *Star Trek* uniform, they're still going hard on that gaylien style. They've got vibrant makeup, an iridescent jumpsuit and a jacket covered in shimmering fabric paint that reads: *They and Them: My Pronouns Are Not a Preference.* As they chat with Joni, their head goes back in a shrieking laugh. More sparkles shed across the barroom floor.

"Earl!" I holler. "Hey, you want a turn? I think we're good up here!"

"Ooh!" Earl squeals, as they grab our bottles and head back. "Actually, I've got this super cute new move I want to try and —"

"Like you're getting off that easy, Ren," Stormé retorts. She snaps shut her pill caddy. "I'm not going to have your clumsy behind bringing down the caliber of the Sunday Showcase."

"I'll be fine." I wave off her concern. "I can always get Tara to slow down the music, right?" I nod toward the DJ booth. Tara pops a bubble loudly in my direction. "I'll take that as a yes."

Stormé flashes me a look. "Fine," she relents. "Just don't mess it up."

Earl fidgets with their platform heels. "For what it's worth," they say, "I thought you did pretty good. Just gotta nail that second turn." As I hop down, they pass my water bottle. "I bet in a couple years you could take an act like that to a pageant at like, Crews, even Bad Times."

"What makes those places so special?" Stormé huffs. She steps toward the back room. Earl and I move quickly after her. In the green room, I watch Stormé squeeze into a lilac fishtail dress and matching plum earrings. Seems like she's made her way into the purples of her monthly rainbow rotation. Of all the performers who come to the Barn's all-ages stage, Stormé is by far the best dressed. I guess that makes sense, since she's also the most experienced. After turning nineteen last fall, she could have moved up to the rest of the drag circuit anywhere else. Thankfully, she seems happy to stay here and keep bossing us around.

"It's just rude," says Stormé, touching up her evening look.

I lean into the mirror to fix my spirit gum and

realize I was supposed to be listening. "Hm?"

She applies a fresh coat of matte lipstick. Its neon colour stands out bright against her ebony skin. "I was *saying*, Ren," Stormé smacks her lips. "All the other kings and queens get to go for pageant titles! And what, we're not allowed, just because we're young?"

"Well, yeah," I answer. I run my fingers along the edges of my jawline. "Most of us couldn't even get through the door at any other bar. Let alone a pageant stage."

"We could host one!" Earl pipes up, spinning on a stool. "A pageant, I mean." They clap their hands toward Stormé. "Oh, I love that colour, such a pretty blue!"

Stormé shakes the tube. "It's periwinkle!"

"Isn't that, like, a shade of blue?" I ask her reflection.

She makes a face at me. "Another word and you'll be the one wearing it tonight."

I laugh, pointing to the *periwinkle* lipstick smudged across her front teeth. Earl starts to giggle and, despite herself, Stormé breaks out into a smile.

My wrist starts to hum. It's my calendar app,

reminding me that I'm supposed to be working on that Bio project. Clover's already started her half of the notes. I snooze the notification just as Joni pops into the dressing room. In a horror-movie style singsong voice, we're warned: "They're *he-ere!*"

With one last deep breath, I push my hair up and shake out my nerves. Showtime.

05 *Closer*

"HOW ABOUT THAT out-of-this-world performance?!"
Stormé takes to the mic, drawing a mix of laughter and
groans from the audience. "What?" she teases. "You try
coming up with new space puns for the fourth show
in a row!" She sends a glittering purple wink off stage
after Earl.

"Nice opener," I whisper. I pat Earl's shoulder as
they pass.

"You're gonna rock it, Ren." Earl pumps their fist.

"Oh, hey!" They spin back toward the stage and call, "Stormé! I got another one! Rock it! You know, like *rocket*?"

"Very nice." Stormé gives an eye roll and the crowd laughs along with her. "Now, get ready to drop back down to Earth ... Because tonight, it's Ren-ing men!"

I wince, but there's no time to complain about puns now.

The lights drop. I tuck my arms against my sides, making sure my binding is still in place. Beads of sweat trickle down to the base of my neck. I take my place at centre stage and let out a shallow breath. A red spotlight flashes. The first few notes of the song thrum in my chest. The whole room is electric with anticipation. On the fourth beat, I snap up my head and the lights go wild. Every eye is on me. But all I feel is the hit of the tempo.

I start to mouth the words as I hit my first turn. Spin once, twice, three times. Something catches my eye, a glint in the darkness. Round glasses reflect the disco ball above.

Clover's here, sitting near the back.

My heart skips and so does my footing. I stumble and lose my place. I recover but just barely, struggling to keep up. What comes after this next bit? I'm not sure I remember. I catch Stormé watching me, brow furrowed. Earl is biting at their nails. I can practically hear Tara's judgemental bubble-gum pop. Maybe Stormé was right, this number needs a little more fine-tuning.

Just when it feels like I'm about to totally bomb, I spot a couple of girls near the front staring hungrily at my half-open shirt. At least my binding tape is holding up. Leaning down, I swing off the stage and snag an ice cube from one of their drinks. I rub it against my lips and then let it trace down the centre of my smooth chest.

The crowd goes wild. My heart is pumping loud, but I keep my face calm. Making my way in spirals around the room, I stroke against shoulders and fall into laps. I make it back to the stage just in time for my final pose. I lap up a wave of applause. But when the lights go up, I don't see Clover anywhere.

I come off stage out of breath. My wrist starts to buzz. It looks like Tara beat Earl to the Insta post this time, tagging @The.Real.Ren in a bird's-eye view of my crowd-pleasing turn. A ton of likes are building up, but one in particular catches my eye — an account named @LikeTheFlower with a profile pic that's a crown of woven clovers. That same account just started following me. My heart soars up so fast it gets stuck in my throat.

My hair prickles as I hug my phone close and scroll through the account. Not many posts, mostly artsy stuff like grey skies or empty alleyways. But I know it's Clover. I recognize a couple of things, like a shot of round wire glasses sitting on her granny's dresser.

A text message slides down onto my screen. It's Clover, asking if I've had a chance to look at the Google Doc she made for our Bio project. I swipe it out of the way. I'll reply when I'm not busy creeping through her profile.

I study the only picture with her face in it. Of

course, it's all artsy and blurry. I pause, my thumb hovering, careful not to tap too quickly and accidentally like the pic.

There's a smack against my shoulder. "That was sickening!" Earl exclaims with a shriek.

"Chill, Earl." I shrug and quickly tuck my phone from view. "This isn't *Drag Race*." Still, I can't help but smile. That was one of the best crowd reactions I've had in a while.

There's a pop next to my ear. Tara shoves past, lugging some equipment from the booth. I try to step out of the way but lose my footing on a patch of especially slippery glitter. I fall back and brace for impact with the grimy, boot-print-covered floor.

Quick hands catch my shoulders. "Nice save, tonight, Don Juan." Stormé pushes me upright. "Hmm." She taps her chin as she leads us toward the green room. "Don Juan? Don Ren? Maybe there's something there ..."

Slipping under Stormé's arm, I sneak another glance at my phone. I freeze. There's a little red heart, right under Clover's burry side profile pic. I must have accidentally liked it! That post is from six months ago. I'm so totally wrecked. That's when I see a little red bubble sitting in my direct-message inbox.

@LikeTheFlower: Hey.

That's it. That's the whole message. What's that even supposed to mean? I'd muse on it longer, but she's seen that I've seen it. I rapidly type the best reply I can come up with.

@The.Real.Ren: Sup?

@LikeTheFlower: NM. Cool show.

I start to wriggle in excitement but quickly bottle it back up when I spot Earl looking. My fingers are getting so sweaty I can hardly type.

@The.Real.Ren: Maybe stick around and say hi next time.

The pounding in my chest starts up again, even louder than when I was on stage. I'm starting to lose my breath. That was the absolute worst thing to say, I'm sure of it. My thumb hovers over the message as I consider deleting it, but it's too late.

She's seen it. And now three little dots are coming up on the screen as she types her reply.

@LikeTheFlower: Maybe I will ☺

06 *Motivation*

I TAP MY FOOT and stare at the clock that sits above Mrs. Burchum's head. The thin second hand seems like it's hardly moving. I'm convinced Mrs. B does something to slow it down. From behind her desk, she glances up at me. I quickly duck my head like I'm focusing on the Math worksheet. When she looks away, I edge up the corner of my sleeve and my stomach does a flip. A message is waiting for me on Insta.

@LikeTheFlower: You ever seen a tardigrade close up? I was reading this article last night, they're actually kind of cute! And horrifying. But the cute kind of horrifying. One sec, I'll send a pic . . .

The bell rings sweet relief. I'm the first one out of my seat. I jump over the legs of sleeping slackers and cut past the keeners lining up to talk with the teacher. The halls are filled with clusters of nervous grade nines and roaming packs of perma-sweaty jocks. My face stays glued to my phone, re-reading Clover's message before starting my reply.

Over the last couple weeks, our messages have grown from one or two words to sentences, to paragraphs, to full-on novels. Talking with her is like having four conversations at once, all on top of each other. She'll start one with an idea she had over breakfast. Next, she's telling me about cumulonimbus clouds or the vibrational properties of different metals. Once, she managed to make me tear up over the history of the toaster oven. Half the time I end up in a Wiki-hole, just trying to keep up.

Last night I was up until almost sunrise, just thinking about texting her. I'm constantly checking her feed for new pictures. I've spent far too much time agonizing over exactly which emojis to use. Is the big smiley too over-eager? The blue heart less weird than the red? Of course, it's always Ren's icon that sits alongside my half of the conversation.

"Hey, Lauri!" someone shouts, way closer than I was expecting. The next thing I know I'm pitched forward into a stack of papers that scatter across the floor. "Geez," Rodger groans. He untangles himself from me. "Text and drive much?"

"Sure, whatever," I mumble. I snatch up my phone and check to make sure the screen's not broken.

"I was actually looking for you." Rodger tries to gather up all his gaudy posters and leaflets before they get trampled. "We're still short staffed on the prom planning team and —"

"Sorry, bud." I step over him as I head toward the cafeteria.

Snaking around the lunch line, I keep my nose firmly pointed toward my phone. Running on instinct, I slip past stoners swapping edibles and rich kids sneaking off to hit their Juuls. I head for my usual spot at the sticky, trash-covered table next to the vending machines.

My stomach grumbles but I can hardly think about food. Clover has already moved on from those weird water bears and just said this really deep thing about baby goats. I want to say something totally deep back. But I'm pretty sure the only thing that makes deep stuff actually deep is doing it without trying. Which is pretty much impossible at this point.

"Listen, Lauri." Rodger suddenly appears next to me. Yellow papers follow behind him like an anti-environmental trail of breadcrumbs. "We both know you could use an extracurricular for university applications. And you keep skipping Spectrum meetings."

"You're still here?" I groan, peeling myself away from my messages to give him an annoyed glare. "You know it's not my scene. Can't you just bug somebody like Stephanie to sign up? She'd bring half the school!"

"Steph? She's way too busy!" Rodger plops down,

brushing aside a handful of empty chip bags and a half-finished strawberry milk. "Seriously, we have no music, no food, no nothing!" He snorts in exasperation. "We don't even have any ideas for the theme!"

"What about . . . prom theme?" I mumble. I want to run over my message to Clover a few more times before pressing send. I get the feeling spelling mistakes would be a turn off.

"Hi, Rod," says a familiar voice. I spin around to see Clover. She is hugging a large binder and two textbooks. "Oh, hey, Lauri." She smiles at me. I feel like melting right onto the tacky cafeteria floor.

"You two know each other?" I manage, trying not to let my voice crack.

"Oh, yeah!" Rodger's braces sparkle. "Clover's on the committee with me!"

"Yep, just us and Mr. Mandelo!" Clover lets out a breathy laugh. "He's the faculty supervisor. Though I'm pretty sure he sleeps through the meetings."

"Eyes open." Rodger shudders. "Really creepy."

Clover cautiously sets her books down and sits

beside us. "Oh, uh, sticky," she grimaces.

"Watch out for gum," I warn her, quickly slipping my phone into my backpack.

"Thanks," she says quietly. She pulls out a small brown lunch bag with a shaky heart drawn on one side.

"What about you two?" asks Rodger. "How'd you meet?"

The blood drains from my cheeks. Dropping from view, I dive face-first into my bag. I try to make it look like I'm digging for change for the vending machine.

"We're lab partners in Bio," says Clover casually. "That reminds me. Lauri?"

"Mhm?" I mumble from the recesses of my backpack.

"Did you get my text?" she asks.

I freeze, a handful of quarters and dimes in my sweaty grip.

"About the Google Doc," says Clover. "Did you have a chance to read it over?"

"Oh!" I pop back up. "Right, totally. Definitely did." I promise myself to check it as soon as I get home.

"Great." She smiles and reaches for her textbook. "Because I was thinking we could actually start with a PowerPoint and then —"

"Here y'all, here y'all!" An obnoxious bellow booms through the cafeteria. I lean back and spot Kyler standing on top of a wobbly table, waving his arms. A hockey jersey sits tied like a cape on his broad shoulders.

"Isn't it supposed to be 'hear ye'?" Clover whispers.

"Hey!" one of the cafeteria workers shouts, waving her fist. "Get down!"

"All rise for a message from King Brian!" Kyler announces. Giggles float through the room. "I said, get up!" A couple of younger kids nervously hop to their feet.

"Are you listening to me?!" The lunch lady throws down her large spoon and swings out from behind the counter. A couple jocks come up from behind and snag her hairnet, managing to distract her with a chase.

Linking their beefy arms, Kyler pulls up Brian. The second bro-dude is decked out in a worn red cape and crown. I think the theatre kids used those props for last year's musical.

Brian briefly surveys his kingdom, pausing on the popular girls' table. "Steph, my princess," he says. He pulls out a cheap plastic tiara that still has a Dollarama sticker on it. "Be my prom date?"

Stephanie squeals and leaps up from her seat. She rushes over and they share a sloppy, wet kiss in front of everyone.

"If he's king," Clover points out, "why's she a princess?"

"Maybe he's her 'daddy,'" Rodger snorts.

"I think I lost my appetite," I groan. "I can't believe people are already doing this whole promposal thing."

"That's why we need to get our shit together!" Rodger slaps his hand down. He peels his palm off the sticky table and wipes it on his jeans. "Sorry for swearing."

"Hard pass," I grumble. "No way I wanna be responsible for those idiots' happiness."

"Well, maybe we can find you another motivation." Clover's dark eyes turn to meet mine, holding my gaze for a few seconds. The hair on the back of my neck stands up.

Rodger coughs loudly. "Uh, Clover," he asks, running his hand through his hair. "Has anybody asked you . . ."

Clover's phone buzzes and she snatches up her textbooks. "Actually, sorry, I just remembered, I have to . . . call Granny." She scampers off.

Rodger's face falls as he watches her go. "Do you think that was because of me?"

I shrug, standing up to head for the back exit. I think I'd be better off getting lunch from the 7-Eleven today.

07 Special Affair

SIPPING AN ENERGY DRINK, I swivel back and forth in my chair. I try to keep my eyes on my laptop but my thoughts wander to the collection of pens scattered across my desk. I should clean those up, maybe put them in a jar . . . I shake my head. I must be procrastinating hard if I'm starting to fantasize about tidying.

There's a loud rattle from my phone buzzing on my desk. Resisting the urge to check if it's Clover, I pick it up and throw it onto the bed in one smooth motion. Just doing that makes me feel accomplished. Look at me! Being responsible! I slip back to my laptop and hop over to Google Docs, finally ready to catch up on our Bio project.

It's been a couple weeks since I promised Clover that I would read the outline. Actually, I told her I had already read it. Same thing, really. When I got home, I told myself I just needed to chill out for a minute. I'd finished a big day of school . . . didn't I deserve a break? I didn't mean to get distracted, but I found this YouTube channel that posts old episodes of 2000s reality TV. The next thing I knew, I was on Season 5 of the original *Queer Eye*.

Things just got busier. Every day, I told myself I'd get to my part of the PowerPoint that night. But there were new trends on TikTok to follow, routines to plan for the Sunday Showcase. Not to mention all my messages to Clover that needed to be researched, crafted and triple-checked before being sent. Now, the presentation is looming, and I can't even remember our topic.

On the plus side, Clover's been at the last two Sunday shows. Last time, she even stuck around for a hot minute. We had maybe awkward, maybe flirty eye contact across the dance floor.

My smartwatch buzzes on its charging dock. I shrug it off and gulp down more energy drink. The fizzy bubbles tickle at first, then burn as they travel down. That's how you know it's good.

The watch buzzes again. And again. Somebody's trying to call me. Who even does that? I snatch up the watch on the fourth ring, ready to tell whoever it is to leave me the hell alone. Don't they know I'm doing my homework?!

I'm expecting some spammer or something, but instead it's Stormé. "Ren. Family meeting, twenty minutes."

I drop my voice low. "Where?"

"VV Boutique on Lansdowne," Stormé tells me. In the background, I can hear Earl whining about something while Tara's unmistakable beats play through a crackling car stereo. "Need a ride?"

I shoot one last look toward my homework. "I'll meet you there."

"And Anita's all pissed at Mikey, even though she's the one who started the whole butt-pads thing to begin with," Earl chatters as they flip through a clothing rack.

"Right, right . . ." I mutter. I check the legs of a pair of black jeans. No luck. They never have slim fits in my size. "Earl, have —"

"Then Mikey made this whole callout post . . ." The wire hangers squeak as Earl rapid-fires through the long-sleeves.

"Earl?" I try again, a little louder.

"But, like, cancel culture is so cancelled." They jump over to the hoodies and sweatshirts. "Like, where's the accountability?" Earl pauses and holds up a bright teal pullover covered in flaking sequins. "Oh, cute!"

"Earl!" I snap, almost dropping a pair of bright white cords onto the slush-covered floor.

Earl runs their hands over the sweater's glittering shoulder pads. "Ren?"

I let out a slow breath. "Did Stormé and Tara get back from parking the van yet?"

"Oh, they're totally here already." Earl points across the store. I follow their finger and spot the other half of our drag family browsing lightly used lingerie.

"Cool." Finally, I find a pair of pants that seem close to my style. I hold them up and grimace as the bottoms run right over the edges of my boots. Meanwhile, the waist looks like it would split me in two. "Ugh!" I groan. "Why is it so impossible to find anything that actually fits?!"

Earl blinks at me. "You could try the little boys' section?"

"Let's just go," I grumble and head for the change room.

It's a cold, wet weekday, which means we've got most of the Value Village to ourselves. We snag three changing stalls in a row. Tara hangs outside, shoving in several pieces of chewing gum and getting ready for the show.

"So I got word to the old queens who run the Barn," says Stormé's shadow from under the stall to my right. "Pitched them Earl's idea."

"Earl had an idea?" I try to sort all the things I picked up. I don't remember collecting this much stuff while browsing.

"I had an idea?" Earl echoes on my left. Their stall floor is a pile of shimmery leggings and sweater-dresses.

"The pageant!" I hear from Stormé's boots on my right. "It took a little convincing. But Joni talked them into giving us the green light. We just have to make it worth their while."

"What's that supposed to mean?" Earl kicks a loose hanger under the edge of their stall and into mine. "They wanna be the judges or something?"

"They want to get paid," Stormé says bluntly.

I pull at a pair of colourful shorts that barely make it halfway up my thighs. "Well, a lot of people want a lot of things."

There's the muffled pop of bubble-gum, followed by a smacking sound. I'm pretty sure that's Tara weighing in.

"That's what I said!" Stormé tosses a bright orange dress over the partition between us. "Good news is, since they let us come in most Sundays anyway, they're waiving rental fees. But if we want the show to go for any longer than our usual set, we've got to make it back in drinks and tips. For that, we need a crowd."

"Well, that's something we can do," I say. I slip on an extra-musty collared shirt. My chest strains against the buttons. I toss it in the *maybe* pile. There's a chance it'll fit when I'm binding.

"Sure." Stormé taps her heel. "Normally, I'd just take care of all the planning. But for something this big, I'm delegating." The lock on her stall clicks open. "Tara's obviously on sound, lights, all the tech stuff."

Tara loudly smacks and pops a bubble in agreement.

"Earl, deco and social," Stormé continues. "Think you can handle that?"

"Yaas!" Earl slams their stall open. I try to loudly roll my eyes.

Sucking in my waist, I struggle against the final button on a corduroy vest. "What about me?" I ask over the door.

"For a proper pageant, we need some competition. Just enough to keep it interesting." I hear the beep of a phone reminder, followed by the quiet click of Stormé's pill caddy. "Ren, you're in charge of finding us new talent."

"Makes sense." I run my hands along the soft velvet of a suit jacket. Finally, something fits perfectly. I grin and hop out of the change room. "A pretty face and a name they recognize should get folks interested."

Earl gives a thumbs up. Tara raises an eyebrow, takes out a massive gum wad and sticks it to the change room door. Stormé looks me over with an expression halfway between amusement and pity. "It's stained," she says, tapping her finger against a splotch on the left shoulder of my perfect fit.

I consider the blemish for a few seconds. "I'll put a pin on it."

There's a buzzing from my bag and Tara kicks it toward me. Fishing out my phone, I find four DMs from Clover telling me about her childhood pet giant snail. Plus one from Mom asking if I'll be home for dinner.

Stormé nods toward my phone. "Somebody dead or something?"

"It's nothing," I say quickly, my face already starting to get warm.

"Ooh, what's their name?" Earl nudges my side, arms full of brightly patterned clothing.

"It's nothing!" I say more firmly, cracking a thin smile. Slipping off my new coat, I follow the others to cash out.

08 Come Undone

HARD RAIN PELTS at the Biology classroom windows. I anxiously tap my pencil. Clover's late. She hasn't been answering my texts. I'm starting to get seriously nervous. Honestly, between drag stuff and keeping up with Ren's DMs, I kind of forgot today was presentation day. If Clover doesn't show, I don't know what I'll do. For now, Stephanie and Brian's bickering is the only thing standing between me and a failing grade.

"So as you dudes can see, the mitochondria are the powerhouse of . . ." Brian turns back. "Next slide, Steph!"

"Just a sec!" Stephanie rapidly types on her laptop. "Just a few finishing touches." She gives a forced smile. I can hear a couple of the first-row kids start whispering.

Shoving his hands into his pockets, Brian leans back on his heels. Even from here, I can spot beads of sweat on his pasty forehead, bright blue in the projector light. "Almost ready, babe?"

"Obviously not!" Stephanie hisses. "I told you we should've done it last night."

One of the guys at the back howls, kicking up his feet. "Tell us all about what you *were* doing last night!"

Stephanie's cheeks go bright pink while everyone giggles and groans. Everyone except Mr. Mandelo. He's slumped back on a stool by the light switch. His eyes are open but I swear I can hear him snoring.

"Shut *up*, Kyler!" Brian puffs up his shoulders.

Kyler drums his hands loudly on his desk. "What're you gonna do about it, stud?"

"I swear," Stephanie glares at Brian. "If you told anyone . . ."

"Oh no!" Kyler keeps teasing. "Has he been a bad boy? Does he need a spanking?"

This time, Brian's the one to go red. Everyone's talking now, jostling in their seats. I keep my eyes fixed on the door, willing Clover to walk through.

A loud cough cuts through the clatter as Mandelo shakes himself up. "Is there a problem?" he asks, pulling at his moustache.

The whole room goes quiet. In a snap, Stephanie slips on a PowerPoint slide that just reads *THE END*. "And that's our presentation on the mitochondria!" she announces with a smile. Taking her hint, Brian starts clapping loudly. He glowers at the rest of the class until everyone else claps too.

"Well done." Mr. Mandelo marks something down on his clipboard and clears his throat. Brian heads to his seat. Stephanie stares daggers into the back of his head as she follows. "Now, who's up next? Ah, Ms. Garber and —"

"Yes! I'm here!" Clover slams through the door, smacking it into the wall. "I'm ready!"

"Ms. Hines." Mandelo snorts, tapping his watch.

Not waiting for another word, Clover runs over to hook up her tablet to the projector cord. I slink my way up beside her to whisper, "Where were you?"

"Finishing *our* project," Clover tells me through her teeth. "I went to do a dry-run last night and found out all your slides were copy-pasted from Wikipedia!"

"Oh," is all I can think to say.

"It's fine. I handled it," Clover grumbles. She points at the keyboard. "Just press the button when I say so."

The projector clicks on and beams down like a spotlight. I hover my finger over the spacebar and find my hand shaking. This is nothing like when Ren takes the stage. I look back at Clover but all I catch is the flash of her glasses as she turns to face the room. She starts talking like someone reading out of a textbook. Ahead, the blank faces of our classmates make my palms start to sweat.

"Next slide!" Clover calls out. I snap back to attention and go to press the button. My hands are so damp, they don't work with the touch screen. I wipe them on my pants and try again. This time, I click too much and end up skipping past several pages of text. Jumping back and forth, I'm totally lost.

Clover steps out from the light with a sigh. "Just let me do it."

"I got this!" I try to sound confident, but it comes out like a squeak. Frantically I click faster, trying to show that I'm not totally useless. Clover pushes my hands aside, but I shove her back. The two of us struggle for control.

"Chick fight!" Kyler shouts from the back. Brian laughs along with him, slapping a high five.

There's a loud snort from Mr. Mandelo. "Is there a problem, ladies?"

"Why are you being so difficult?" Clover searches my face in confusion.

"It's fine!" I stammer. "Everything is fine!" Stumbling back, I slip. Clover manages to snag the tablet so I don't send the whole thing flying. Still, there's a loud snap and everything goes dark.

The projector starts to hum and the screen reads *NO SIGNAL*. A loose, frayed cord sits hanging from the podium. The other half hangs from the tablet in Clover's hands.

I step forward, hoping it's not as bad as it looks. There's a spark from the projector booth and the sound of something fizzling. "Uh . . ." I murmur. "Yep, that's not good."

A heavy shadow looms over us both. "Ms. Hines, Ms. Garber." Mandelo grimaces. "Do you feel this is an appropriate way to treat school equipment?"

Clover stares down at her hands. "Sir, I — I didn't —" She pulls the tablet to her chest. "I don't know —"

"You don't know?" Mr. Mandelo waddles over to inspect the damage, hands on his hips. "We'll need to call the principal," he grumbles. "Likely your parents as well . . ."

Behind Clover's round glasses, her brown eyes go wide. The kids at the back start whispering and laughing. Stephanie and some of the other girls start to giggle.

"Somebody's in trouble," Kyler sings in the back.

"I've never known a young lady to be so clumsy," Mr. Mandelo grumbles. Clover's lips start to tremble. There's a terrible knocking sound in my chest, rising to pound in my ears. I manage to catch Mr. Mandelo saying something about a failing grade.

There's a loud smack as Clover's tablet falls to the floor, the half-cord curling like a limp snake. The classroom door hits against the wall as she runs out.

"Drama queen!" someone calls after her. There's another ripple of laughter.

Mr. Mandelo just shakes his head. "That young lady has an attitude problem."

"*Her* attitude?!" I snap, waving at the peanut gallery at the back. "What about those guys?!"

Mr. Mandelo's moustache bristles like an angry caterpillar. "That tone is hardly appropriate —"

"*You're* hardly appropriate!" My face is burning red hot.

"Defensive much?" I hear Kyler snicker. "What is she, your girlfriend?"

"Dyke!" Brian coughs loudly. Stephanie pokes him in the side, but doesn't say anything.

"Ms. Garber," Mandelo starts again, but I'm not sticking around.

"Shut up!" I shout. I grab Clover's tablet from the floor. "All of you, just shut up!" I yank loose the busted projector cord and a wail of laughter follows me into the hall.

09 *Runaway*

NO SIGN OF CLOVER in the hallway. I go for my phone but then stop. Would it make sense for Ren to message her right now? And would she even want to talk to Lauri?

As I push through a doorway into the upper stairwell, my eyes drift to the thin windows. A thousand fingerprints hang smudged against a grey sky. It's that time of spring when everything just looks dead. At least the hail's stopped, for now.

I try a text as Lauri. From below, there's a soft buzzing sound. I send another. There it is again. I lean over the railing and spot Clover curled up under the stairs. She sniffles loudly, clutching her phone. She types something, pauses, then deletes it.

I drop an arm down and give a lopsided wave. "Sup?"

Clover pulls her phone close and looks up at me like a deer in headlights. "I got your tablet?" I say, holding it out towards her.

I try to drop down all smooth but get stuck on the railing's rubbery grip. I nearly land face-first on the concrete floor. Brushing myself off, I ask, "You good?"

Clover purses her lips and pushes back against the wall. I slump to the floor and slide the tablet toward her. Reluctantly, she takes it. "Thanks," she mumbles.

"No worries," I answer. Clover stays quiet. I start picking at my nail beds. After what feels like forever, I ask, "Do you wanna talk about —?"

"No," she says flatly.

"Cool, cool, cool." I suck in air through my teeth. I pull at my shoelaces and mutter, "Just, you know, I'm sorry or whatever."

"What's that?" She sneaks a look toward me.

"I'm sorry," I say again, a little louder.

Clover takes off her glasses and breathes on the lenses. "For what?"

"For . . . I don't know." I kick out one leg. "Messing around. Getting you in trouble." I sigh. "I didn't mean to space on the whole presentation thing. I just . . . got busy."

"I'm busy too."

My stomach sinks in a pit of guilt. "Right."

She pinches the edge of her shirt around the lenses, tracing circles and checking for specks. "It's whatever," she declares. "I wasn't planning on keeping College Bio on my transcript anyway."

I blink in surprise. "You're not mad?"

Looking satisfied, Clover slips on the frames. "There's still twenty minutes before next period." She raises her eyebrows at me.

The pit in my stomach spins into a whirlpool. I swallow my nerves and ask, "Feel like a Slurpee run?"

Clover grimaces. "I don't really drink those things."

"You haven't had one the way I make them." I reach out my hand and nod toward the fire-exit. That door's alarm has been busted since before I even started grade nine. "Don't worry. Nobody'll even notice we're gone."

Clover squeezes her eyes shut, giving her head a hard shake. "What did you say was in here again?"

"A bit of everything." I shrug. I drop a couple toonies on the counter as the sketchy old guy rings us out at the cash. Once he's got his back turned, I whisper, "The real secret is a splash of the Red Bull they keep near the back."

Clover scrunches up her nose. "Gran never lets me have that stuff."

"Doesn't that make it taste even better?" I grin.

I don't have enough to pay for two drinks, so we take one to share and blow the rest of my change on five-cent candies. Chewing on rock-hard gummy sharks, we lean against the wall of the 7-Eleven and watch cars roll by. A big truck roars through a puddle on the other side of the street, totally soaking a couple of older kids. Laughing at their dripping faces, I elbow Clover to join in, but her eyes are glued to her phone.

"Texting somebody?" I ask, trying not to let my voice shake. Is she waiting for Ren to message her? Or, worse, is she talking to someone else the way she talks to him?

"Just keeping an eye on the time," Clover says, taking another sip. She winces and smacks her tongue, then goes back for more. "Math's next period. If I miss the first bit, I'll be totally lost for the rest."

"We're fine," I tell her. "Don't stress."

"Easy for you to say," Clover huffs. "In University Math, people actually give a crap."

I swallow hard on a half-chewed gummy and feel my

CONFESSIONS OF A TEENAGE DRAG KING

cheeks warming. "Fine." I shuffle my feet. "Let's go."

"Wait." Clover pulls on my sleeve. It sends a shiver up my arm. "We don't have to rush."

We compromise by heading toward the alleyway and take the long way back to school.

"I'm sorry," Clover says, studying her shoes.

"What are you sorry for?" I take a long sip until I'm hit with wicked brain-freeze.

"For running off." She nudges me, linking our arms. "I don't like being put on the spot like that."

"Mr. Mandelo's a turd." I rub my temples. "Don't listen to that boomer. Stupid cable's probably like ten bucks on Amazon."

"It's not just him." Clover kicks pebbles into a rainbow-slick puddle. "It's everybody. All of them, staring, laughing at me . . . I hate that."

"It's not easy being the new kid." I offer her a sip but Clover just shrugs. "Hey," I ask, "are you going to prom with Rodger?"

She blinks up at me. "Am I . . . what?"

My palms are warm against the cold Slurpee cup.

I can feel its colourful slush starting to melt inside. "That's the only reason I can think of that you'd sign up for that stupid prom committee."

"You think I want to go with *Rodger*?!" She starts to crack up.

"Well, I . . ." I can't help but start laughing too. "What am I supposed to think?! That you just *love* planning prom for a school you'd never even been to?"

Clover grips her sides and nearly slips on the slushy road. She falls against a graffiti-covered door, pulling me along with her and the two of us giggle like little kids. Eventually, we're not laughing about anything except the fact that we're laughing so hard. Every time we start to catch our breath, we catch each other's eyes and the whole thing starts again.

"Whew, okay," Clover says at last. She shivers and brushes her thick curls aside. "No, I'm not going with Rodger. He's nice but, uh, not really my *type*."

"That's a relief," I admit as I wipe my cheeks.

"Is it?" Clover glances at me. Just as I'm getting my breath back, it catches in my throat. "Prom committee's an extracurricular," she explains. "Looks good on applications. I haven't heard back from any schools yet, but every little bit helps."

"Schools? Like, university?"

"I'm hoping for a scholarship." Clover brushes off her shoulders. "My folks . . . Well, I want to be able to pay my own way, you know?"

Clover starts heading back towards the school. I drop our empty Slurpee cup on the ground to follow. She stops and gives me a look. Sheepishly, I go back to collect my litter.

"Plus," she pokes me. "It's fun, caring about stuff. You might try it sometime."

"I care about things!" I crumple the cup and shove it in my back pocket.

"Like?" She raises her brows.

"Things! Lots of things!" I stammer. I dig in my pocket and find one of the five-cent candies. "So that's it? Just building up those extra credits?"

"It was that or join the volleyball team." Clover pushes her glasses up her nose. "And, well . . ."

"What, you're not the athletically gifted type?" I try to flip it into my mouth but it lands on the ground with a splat. A few seconds later, the smushed candy is joined by thin droplets of rain tracing along the pavement.

"You could say that." Clover shields her hair from the drizzle.

"I'm shocked!" I give an exaggerated gasp. "It's not like I'm in gym with you or anything!"

"Hey!" She pushes me with her hip and nearly knocks me into a fresh puddle. We both break into laughter again as we chase each other toward the school parking lot.

10 *Way Back*

I TAKE QUICK STEPS from the streetcar, pulling down my hood. I should've waited until I was at the Barn before applying my mascara beard. Droplets cling along my bangs from the cold Sunday morning drizzle.

My wrist buzzes. I wipe the watch-face with my sleeve and scan the message from our drag family group chat.

Earl: Just got us a table ☺ What's everyone's ETA?

I peer through the mist. Glad Day's pink awning

is still a few blocks away. We were supposed to meet at the bookshop-café a half-hour ago for a pageant-planning meeting. In true drag fashion, everyone's running late.

Stormé: Be there in five. @Ren, you do the schedule yet? Tara needs all music asap.

Tara: 🎶🎧

I grit my teeth. I promised to have the set list sorted by now. I even set up a whole online application thing, but haven't had a chance to check it. I pull out my phone to swipe to my email app, just barely managing to remember the password. Once I get in, panic rises in my chest like steam from the street.

Inbox: 59 Unread.

I scroll, hoping at least a few are spammers or scam artists. No luck. Nearly every one comes from a performer applying for the show we're hosting *this* weekend! Some are even multiple acts. I hop into the group chat, typing as quick as I can.

Ren: Are we really sure inviting a bunch of strangers is a good idea?

Ren: Just saying. Hosting all these amateurs, isn't that opposite the whole point of the show?

Somebody had to say it. People already don't take us seriously as an all-ages show. I don't get how having a ton of baby-gays show up is going to help. I watch as each of their icons pop up and read my message. Stormé starts to type, then stops. Tara sends a shrug emoji and goes offline. Finally, there's a reply.

Earl: We all had to start somewhere.

Earl: Just like when you joined, right @Ren?

Stormé: Let's talk about this IRL.

I clench my jaw as I start to formulate a response. Ahead, I barely notice the ring of a storefront doorway. Next thing I know, I smack into somebody's side. My phone flies and clatters onto the wet sidewalk.

"Hey —!" I start to protest, until I look up.

Clover grins back at me, dimples forming on her cheeks. "Hey, yourself."

I try to untangle my tongue and push out a breath. I remind myself of who I am right now. In my best Ren-voice, I ask, "Where you headed?"

"Nowhere," she answers. She opens an umbrella before scooping up my phone. As she passes it back, her fingers brush against mine. "Mind if I join you?"

The streets of the Village are busy as ever. Cars splash past as bike-couriers haul food to condos and office buildings. We pass a couple kids huddling under the scaffold of a sex-shop-turned-bank. I can still see an outline on the window where it used to say *XXX*, pasted over with a rainbow sticker.

"Seriously, what're you doing out here?" I pull my jacket tighter. "You really just walk around?"

"I like to people-watch," Clover replies. She pauses at a flower shop window and her words fog against the display. "There's a lot to notice, when you stop to look."

She catches me watching her reflection. I don't look away. "See anything you like?" I ask.

"That person working checkout." Clover nods toward someone with an apron and a sharp undercut. "They're into one of the baristas at the Starbucks over there. Crushing pretty hard, I'd guess."

Before I can ask, she points to a series of coffee cups resting along the windowsill. "Orders two cups a day but never finishes them. Never talks to the barista either, from what I've seen."

"Maybe they're just nervous," I offer, nibbling at the inside of my cheek.

"Are you ever?" She lifts her face toward me, then her gaze wanders to the tall, brick walls of the Barn. "Nervous, I mean. All those people watching you . . ."

"What, on stage?" I scoff. "Honestly, first time I ever saw a show, just being in the audience was terrifying!"

"Oh?" she asks with a hint of surprise. "Then why'd you go on?"

"I didn't mean to," I admit. "That whole day was just really, really weird." I trail off but Clover stays quiet.

Even though part of me knows better, I let out a little more of the story. "My mom woke me up. She used to let me sleep in on Sundays. But that morning she came in, sat on the edge of my bed. Said we needed to talk."

"Mm, never good." Clover inches closer so the umbrella covers us both.

"Seriously," I sigh. "The way she was talking, I thought somebody had died. She told me it wasn't my fault, that no one could have seen this coming."

Clover pulls me aside as the florist steps out of the shop and passes quickly. "Seen what coming?"

I watch as the undercut heads two doors down, into the Starbucks. "She'd fallen in love with somebody. By the time I got dressed, Dad was already at the door. Bags packed." Despite the umbrella, the wet air seeps through my coat and makes me shiver. "Never was the touchy-feely type, I guess."

We both study the street. "That sucks," Clover says eventually.

"Yeah." I let out a misty chuckle. "Mom tried to talk but I was just too pissed off. Next thing I knew, I was outside. Just caught the first bus I saw. Hadn't even brushed my teeth."

Clover pushes her chin toward the Barn. "And you ended up there?"

Just the sight of it steadies me a little. "Yeah," I nod toward the bar. "I figured everything would be closed on Sunday. But that place had music playing. Inside was this kid, younger than me even, rocking out a lip-sync in a mesh top and a full-on Spock wig!"

"Earl Grey." Clover's laugh is warm on my cheek. Another shiver runs down my spine. This time, it's not because I'm cold.

"They were doing auditions," I tell her. "New acts for the Sunday Showcase. But Stormé was a tough judge."

"So, what?" Clover raises her brows. "You just walked on stage and got the spot?"

"No, I tried to run!" I shake my head and lean back. "Earl found me before I could head off. Had Joni warm me up a tea. Then Stormé came through and asked for my song. I just said the first one that came to mind and Tara had it on hand."

"Lucky," mutters Clover. She pushes back her curls before drifting a hand toward mine.

"I guess . . ." My own voice feels strangely far away. "Thing is, Dad always wanted me to be this girly-girl.

When I couldn't do that, it just felt like I was nothing. But when that music hit . . . I was . . . I felt . . ."

Clover intertwines our fingers and squeezes. "Like you could be anything?"

"Yeah," I murmur. "Pretty soon, Stormé helped me design a full routine." A laugh fills my chest as I remember. "Oh, and then Earl shaved my head! Kept my bangs, though. I thought Mom would flip if I came home totally bald."

"Did she?" asks Clover. Down the block, the florist comes scurrying back, fresh coffee in hand.

I think a few seconds. "Actually, no. Didn't ask about my new 'youth group' either. Caught up in her own drama, I guess."

Before I can say any more, there's a hum from my watch. More notifications from the group chat, asking where I am. They want to get started.

Clover's thumb gently strokes against mine. "Something important?"

Sliding my phone from my pocket, I use my spare hand to type.

Ren: Something came up.

Ren: Sorry. Catch you next time.

Before they can protest, I hop back to the email. I send out a mass reply, saying when and where to go. Whoever shows up, shows up. We can sort them in person and see if there's any worth having on stage.

I slide my phone onto mute and turn back to Clover. "Nope. Lead the way."

11 Solutions

@LikeTheFlower: And the whole book was in sans-serif font!! Why even bother publishing it???

My backpack slaps against me as I hurry down Church Street. I'm trying to read Clover's latest message, but I also can't be late. After skipping our last meeting, I know the family's not going to be pleased if I'm late for the pageant!

Before I get a chance to answer Clover, I run into a wall of people. I look up to find the Barn has a line that stretches from the entrance around the block. Shoving through shoulders and stepping on toes, I make it inside. I give a nod to Joni as I edge along the mess of sweaty bodies and walls of piled coats, heading for the back.

I push at the door to the dressing room but it hardly budges. After a couple more shoves, I spill inside. The green room is packed. Baby queers glob around the mirrors as they patch crepe hair and stuff bras. I don't recognize anyone until I spot Stormé elbowing a path toward me.

"What . . ." she wheezes, practically drowning in hairspray as one queen sets a wig that looks as hard as a bicycle helmet. " . . . the hell is going on?!"

"Uh . . ." I look around the room. "Big turnout, eh?"

"*Not* cute." Stormé hauls me back through the door and pulls me up to the DJ booth. Earl is crouched on the floor, touching up their pointy ears with a compact. Tara side-eyes me before popping in a stick of gum and slipping on headphones.

"We've spent a month promo-ing this event!"

Stormé is out of breath, her eyeliner smeared. "Earl's been blasting social media. Tara's been rewiring half the speakers in this place. Today, I literally ran down the block to convince the Queens at Crews to come by before their own show!"

"And?" I ask, dropping my bag. I fish out my new-to-me blazer. The stain never really came out, but I don't think anyone will notice.

"And where have you been?!" Stormé leans over to fix her makeup in Earl's mirror. "We show up for set-up and the dressing room's already overrun. Plus, folks still at the door. And all saying they're in the show?!"

"Maybe this is good, right?" Earl gives a hopeful smile. "If they all got in, I can't imagine how many you had to turn down!" Their ears are uneven but it doesn't feel like the time to mention it.

"Right." I peek over Tara's booth. I spot a few of the performers running their moves on the stage. From up here, it looks more like a bunch of Muppets falling over each other. "About that . . ."

"I knew it." Stormé shakes her head. "You had one job, Ren. Look over the applicants and pick a *few* to let into the show. But you just couldn't be bothered, could you?"

"It's not like that!" I turn to Earl but they start fiddling with their phone. Stormé flips her golden wig as she takes in the scene below. I start to feel my face go warm. "Well, if you knew I'd mess it up, why'd you make me do it?!"

"Because we're a team, Ren." Stormé's shoulders slump. Glitter from her yellow dress mists the floor. "A family."

"But, like, you could've checked on it." I start to set my binding and pull together my outfit. "You know sometimes I miss stuff. I'm working on a lot right now!"

"And we aren't?" Stormé taps her nails along the edge of the booth. "Running deco, working lights, building hype, getting ready to MC —" She clenches her fist. "God, I'm supposed to MC this madness! How am I even going to do that?" She swivels toward me.

"Tell me you at least got together a schedule?"

"Well, not exactly." I button my shirt. It's still a little tight around the chest.

Stormé clutches at her cheeks. "Do we even have any judges?"

"Was I supposed to be doing that too?" I sneer. Stormé just stares. I realize she's serious. "Oh, uh, sorry. I didn't get that memo."

There's a knock against the stair railing behind us. "Uh, hey?" Joni pokes her head in. "People getting kinda antsy. Y'all gonna start soon?"

Stormé looks ahead, her eyes vacant. "I don't know . . ."

"Well, do you know when you're gonna know?" Joni glances back toward the bar. "Because a lot of people are asking . . ."

"I said, I don't know." Stormé pinches her nose. "Sorry. Just give us a minute."

Joni sets down a couple bottles with a shrug before leaving us to ourselves. Stormé grabs one of the waters and practically downs the whole thing in one gulp.

"Done!" Earl pops up, tapping their phone. There's a buzz at my wrist, a new message in our chat. "I got into the pageant email — sorry, Ren, but the password was super weak. I got everyone's name and bios. Now, they're in a doc. Tara, I'm sending you a Spotify playlist of their music."

Tara gives a thumbs-up and bobs along to the beats blasting from those massive headphones.

"For judging," Earl flashes us a spreadsheet before flipping to Instagram. "I got everyone's socials. We'll tag the acts as they go up, then the crowd can vote with likes and comments!"

I scrunch my face. I could've done all that. "Won't that kinda skew it for whoever's already popular?"

Stormé lifts a manicured nail toward me. "You, hush! Earl, this is amazing!"

"No prob." Earl shrugs. "The show must go on, right?"

Stormé claps her hand around Earl's shoulder. "The show must go on!" She nudges Tara, who gives a nod and starts up the speakers.

"The show must go on!" I try to chime in. But Stormé's already moving past me down into the fray.

Earl follows, stopping briefly to give me a pat. "Thanks for doing what you could," they tell me as they slip something into my palm. It's a small Star Trek pin. "This should cover the spot on your coat."

"Right," I mumble as they leave me in the booth.

I turn to Tara, who just glares back and loudly pops a big pink bubble. I shove the last of my stuff back into my bag. "See you later."

12 Lips

AN ELBOW SHOVES against my back and pushes me against the hard corner of the stage. Everything is a sea of noise. I can hardly hear Stormé's banter with the crowd.

The lights drop. The music dips. A shiver runs across the room. Clad in flowing, near-translucent white, a figure shimmers into view. Glowing in blacklight, they hold, letting tension build. When the beat hits, they pose, pose, sashay. The room goes wild.

Most of these amateurs act like they're the next RuPaul or Lady Bunny, without any of the follow through. But some . . . For the first time, it hits me. I'm not just up against Earl and the few one-timers who come in for the Barn's slow nights. This is real competition.

There's a tap on my shoulder. "Not now, Earl!" I shrug off another tap before I turn. "Oh. It's you."

Clover nods, having to shout over the music. "Ren, can we talk?!"

My name on her lips makes my heart race. I blink and open my mouth, hoping the right words will spill out. Just then, I spot a tall butch carrying a handful of cocktails through the crowd. They catch their foot on a stray heel and the drinks go flying — right in Clover's direction.

Without thinking, I grab her arms and spin. Flecks of ice and juice splatter against the back of my coat. Clover is pinned against a speaker. Her wide eyes look back at me. Pulsing music runs through us both. The edge of her fingers pull me in. Our faces are so close.

Her breath traces my mouth. I could just . . .

"Now wasn't that just *haunting*!" Stormé laughs as she takes the stage. The music quiets down as she builds up the next act.

Clover runs her hand along my sticky shoulder. "Your jacket."

"Now, friends, foes and all in-between," Stormé flashes me a knowing look. "Put your hands together for the one, the only —!"

I shrug off the coat. "It was stained anyway."

"Ren!" Stormé sings out, getting the crowd to cheer as the lights dim.

I let my jacket drop and swing on stage. Giving a nod to Tara in the booth, I remind myself, *The show must go on.*

My first few steps flirt with the beat. I roll my shoulders, picking up the tempo. Just me and the music, like always. I ride the rhythm higher and higher until nothing else matters.

In the back, cameras flash. I blink, seeing spots. Suddenly, I'm closer to the edge of the stage than I meant to be. I almost step right off the platform. I play like it was on purpose, but I can practically feel Stormé shaking her head.

The spotlight lifts for a second and I'm met with an ocean of faces. They're talking, laughing, milling about. Some are singing tunelessly along to the song. My song. Then I spot Clover waving down Joni for a drink. She's not even watching.

Cold sweat runs down the back of my neck. I try to shake it off. I'm Ren. I don't get nervous. I get inspired. Falling back into the beat, I step down from the stage. On purpose this time. The spotlight follows as I twist through the crowd. I tap Clover's shoulder. She turns back and I flash her a wink as I hoist myself onto the bar.

The song, my song, goes into its breakdown. I strut across the bar rail. "Dude!" Joni starts to shout, but the words get drowned out. Everyone loses it, shouting and grabbing at me as I go. I spin back to Clover and reach down to take her hand.

"What are you doing?!" she gasps.

"Trust me!" I pull her up into a twirl. She slips on the wet counter and grabs onto my shirt. Buttons go flying.

"I —" She dips, taking a step back.

I pull her into my arms. "Kiss me!"

There's a cold splash across my face. My eyes are shocked open. Clover is holding an empty glass in her hand. She adjusts her glasses, passes the drink back down to one of the shocked bystanders and hops down. Someone starts to laugh. Soon the whole room is howling. Cameras flash. My song comes to an end and I stand there, soaked, trying to process what happened.

I catch a familiar squeal and look up. I think I recognize someone. In fact, I know I do. It's Stephanie and . . . Kyler? What are they even doing here?

Everything goes in slow motion. My face feels heavy. Juice drips from my hair. I'm suddenly super aware of everything. My clothes are damp and too tight. I never noticed how itchy this fake beard is. I must look like a total clown. It's so obvious now. I'm just Lauri, making a fool of herself. Playing dress-up in second-hand dad clothes.

Joni pulls me off the bar and throws me past the crowd. The bottoms of my shoes stick to the floor. My back wet with sweat and melting ice, I slump upstairs and land on the floor of the DJ booth. Tara gives me an annoyed glare but gets back to work. The show must go on.

Rainbows flicker across the ceiling. The disco ball slowly turns. The music ended long ago. Maybe if I lie here long enough, I'll just sink through the floor.

There's the sound of a door closing. Heavy heels click across the tacky floor. "Any updates yet?" Stormé's voice is scratchy and worn.

"Votes still coming in," Earl answers. "Next time, I'll try to figure it out sooner so we can announce at the end of the show."

"Ha. Right." Stormé lets out a rough cough. "Next time."

My head lolls to the side. "Is it over?" I ask.

Stormé gives me cold look but, before she can get a word in, there's a bursting sound from near the bar. I roll my head back and my cheek lands in a wet spot on the floor.

"Fabulous!" exclaims one of two round, bald men with white goatees. "Utterly fabulous!"

"Never seen anything like it!" agrees the other, slightly shorter man, clapping his large hands. "Especially not from such young chickens!"

Joni steps out from behind the bar. "Stormé, everyone, this is Oliver and Oliver. The owners of the Barn."

"Oh, of course!" Stormé takes a large step, hand outstretched. "It's so good to meet you —"

"And here's our little star of the show!" The taller Oliver bends down to take my hand and give it a firm shake. "Completely hilarious. Couldn't have been timed better!"

"Everyone's so worried about being PC these days," the shorter Oliver agrees. "It's refreshing to see drag that's not afraid to be funny!"

"Um." I stare up, my brain still struggling to turn on.

Joni reaches into an overflowing tip jar, pulling out wads of fives, tens, even twenties. "What'd I tell you? These folks know how to pull in a crowd."

"Our best profit in months." The taller Oliver beams. He finally turns to Stormé. "We can't wait to see what you pull off next!"

"Shall we say, next month?" asks the shorter one.

Sandwiched by Olivers, Stormé stammers and backs toward the stage. "You want us to do this again?!"

Stomping footsteps come down from the DJ booth. Tara doesn't say a word, just tosses something that catches me in the gut. Opening my palm, I find my smartwatch. It's buzzing like wild. Before I can check it, Earl gives me a twisted grimace. "The Insta-votes. Ren, I think you won."

13 When It's Over

THE BACK OF MY HEAD rests against a hard cement wall. A dry ache pulses behind my eyes. Last night feels like a terrible dream.

Curled up in the crawlspace below the stairs, I listen to the slap of wet sneakers and Monday morning gossip echo down the school halls. Everyone's off to first-period classes. I thought I might catch Clover here. But, nope.

My watch hums. I force myself to look. It could be her.

Of course, it's not. Just another wave of notifications. A video of my failed performance — complete with Clover splashing me in the face — has gone viral. Insta, TikTok, Twitter, YouTube. Pretty much the whole internet has seen it.

What's wild is that a lot of people are coming for Clover. They're accusing her of being a straight girl who wasn't going along with the bit. There's even a petition going around, trying to ban her from all the gay bars in the city.

As I desperately swipe away the endless comments and tags, I get a message. It's the family group chat.

Earl: Results are in. Posting now. Congrats, @Ren.

Great. Just perfect. I knew voting by likes and comments was a bad idea, but I never thought it would go this sideways.

The first morning bell feels like a hammer to the back of my head. I groan and roll onto the ground. I *so* don't want to go to class today. Stephanie's the one who posted the original vid. She has to have figured out who Ren really is. And if she knows, everyone knows. I'd be better off just transferring to another school. I wonder if Mom and Nathan would let me fake my own death.

The second bell rings. I pull myself up off the ground like a zombie in a bad horror movie. I shrug on my backpack and drag my way to class as the national anthem starts crackling over the ancient speaker system.

The morning grinds on slowly. Still, not slow enough. For once, I wish the classroom clocks would just stand still. Madame Dorit hands back our mid-term essays. Mine lands on my desk with a big C+, covered in illegible red pen scribbles. I can't even be bothered to stress. The bell rings again and I shudder. It's time for gym.

My stomach twists into a million knots. My hands cramp up as I try to lace my sneakers. I watch the gym doors with the corners of my eyes. Clover is bound to be here any second. I don't know what I'm going to do. Does she know yet, about Ren? Well, me? Have people told her? What am I supposed to say?

"When were you gonna tell us?!" Morgan hops over, nearly knocking me into the bleachers.

I feel my face draining. "Um, you mean . . ."

"You're friends with her, right?" Sara swoops around from the other side. "Did you know?"

"No way." Devon appears, wrapping up a lap. "Or she'd have shown up to record it first!"

A sharp whistle cuts through our conversation. Ms. Dees waves from across the gym. "Walk and talk, people!"

I drag my feet along the long red line that runs in a circle on the skid-marked floor.

"Seriously, you can tell us," Morgan starts up again, following close behind me. "It's not like we're going to tell anyone."

"Not anyone who doesn't already know, anyway," Sara adds.

I pick up my pace. "I really don't know what you're talking about."

"Told you." Devon spins and jogs backward. "I bet Steph's getting mad followers off that video of Clover. I wonder if she monetized it."

That stops me in my tracks. "Wait, you're talking about —"

"That'd be the smart thing," Sara agrees. "I think even old Mandelo's seen it by now."

Another whistle from Dees calls us to circle up. I follow the trailing whispers as Morgan and the others hurry off.

The cafeteria is packed and rumours are flying. Everyone's seen the video. I'm pretty sure even the lunch ladies are gossiping about it. The room buzzes like a beehive. Or a wasp nest.

"I heard that guy was her ex," says a burnout leaning by the microwave, eating half-frozen mac and cheese. "She had to move schools to get away from him!"

"Um, except obviously that wasn't a real guy," answers a band geek as she picks salad from her braces. "Was this her coming out or something? Maybe we should be being supportive."

"Smells like clout chasing to me," mutters one

of the girls from the wrestling team. She does lunges while waiting in the cafeteria line. "I bet the whole thing was staged."

I push through to my usual place and spot Stephanie. She sits on a table and takes questions like she's at a press conference. "Yes, you in the back." She waves toward a cluster of grade nines who all talk at once. "Yes, I was there celebrating my dear friend's sweet seventeen." She leans down to give Kyler a pat on the shoulder.

A tall kid in a striped sweater waves a phone. "Will you take a selfie with me?" he asks, already leaning back for a pic.

"All right, all right." Brian shoves his way through, carrying a big pink smoothie. "That's enough questions!"

There's a collective whine. Stephanie waves off her fan club as she takes the drink. She smacks a wet kiss on Brian's cheek.

"Makes you kinda sick, doesn't it?" asks a voice next to me. I find Rodger waiting at the trash table.

"Rod, buddy!" I swallow down my guilt and drop my bag. "You seen Clover?"

"As if," he huffs as he unzips his lunch. "I'll be surprised if she doesn't switch schools again."

"Right." I fish out some change to get a chocolate bar for lunch. But it gets stuck halfway down the vending machine. Seems about right.

"It just sucks." Rodger sulks as he watches Stephanie and Brian. It looks like the pair are having some kind of argument. Stephanie shakes the smoothie in Brian's face like she's threatening to dump it. "How can someone so smart do something so stupid?"

"What, you mean Clover?" I give the machine a good shove. "I wouldn't say it's her fault . . ."

"Obviously not!" Rodger sneers, then bites into a crustless sandwich. "You know, we were supposed to have prom committee today. But she's not even sure she wants to do it anymore!"

"You talked to her?" I ask, digging into my pockets. I don't have enough to try for another bar. "Did she say anything about that guy in the video or . . ."

"We had Biology this morning, but she didn't show." Rodger balls up the waxy wrap that held his sandwich. "So I texted to ask if I could bring over her homework later."

"Wait . . ." I look up with a start. "She transferred to your class?"

Rodger stands to pack up the last of his lunch. "Hey," he shrugs toward me. "You know anything about what was really down with Clover and that video?"

"No!" I say, probably too quickly. "Why would I know anything?"

Rodger's eyes linger on me for a few seconds. "Right," he mutters. "Later, Lauri."

As Rodger heads to the exit, behind me I hear two muffled thumps. Looking over my shoulder, I spot Brian fishing out something from the vending machine. "Sweet!" He smiles to his buddies, holding up his prize. "Double bars!"

14 Of Only

SHUFFLING ACROSS MY BEDROOM in my socks, I slide to the beats pumping from my mini speaker. Turn, strike a pose, snap. I pause to check the photo and crop out the background of dirty laundry and piled textbooks.

I had myself prepped to actually study. Even made flashcards and spread them out all over my bed, the way people do in movies. Instead, somehow, I found my way into my binder and a carefully crafted mascara beard.

I take another set of thirst-selfies, beauty filters turned up.

I'd normally be in my drag look anyway. Around now, we're usually prepping for the Sunday Showcase, running rehearsals and finishing sound check. Weirdly, the family chat's been dead silent. Stormé has hardly said anything about our next show. She's probably stressing over planning another pageant, or just giving up altogether. It's strange for Earl to go quiet too. But maybe they just got tired of the way Tara and I always leave them on read.

I go for another snap but my phone vibrates in my hand. It's been more than a week since that video went viral and my notifications are still blowing up. I've untagged myself from everywhere I could find. But now people keep sliding into my DMs. Everyone except the one person I want to talk to.

Clover has completely stopped messaging Ren. To be fair, I haven't sent anything either. Every time I try, my drafts seem whiny or, worse, basic. I don't know how it felt so easy before.

It doesn't help that Clover seems to have lost interest in hanging with Lauri. She barely looks at me when passing in the hall. She's always busy during lunch, too, hanging with Rodger and his stupid prom committee. After transferring into Rodger's mixed-level Bio class, Clover somehow got out of gym for the rest of the semester too. I heard Morgan say it was because of some medical condition. Who knows if that's true. I guess I got too boring for her after all.

"Knock, knock!" My door starts to push open.

"Mom!" I shout. I dash to block her. "Don't come in!"

"And why not?" she asks. She holds steady on the other side.

"I'm — I'm studying!" I shove down my bangs and desperately search for something to hide my face, a scarf, a turtleneck, anything! I nab a mildew-crusted towel off the back of my chair and rub it fiercely against my cheeks. I check in the mirror. Now there's just a big smear running down my chin.

"I know you're working hard," Mom chuckles. Her fingers edge around the door. "But I brought you a special snack!"

". . . Cookies?" I dare a small peek.

"A *healthy* snack, Lauri," Mom takes her chance and throws herself forward, pushing me back. I scramble to the bed. "Apple slices and peanut butter, your favourite!"

"Yeah, when I was five," I mutter, hiding behind a textbook.

"I thought you had your youth group today." She picks up a few loose socks and turns up her nose at an empty Slurpee cup. I stay quiet, waiting her out. "You know, kiddo . . ." she says, lingering at the edge of my bed. "If you're having feelings, maybe about Nathan moving in, we can talk about it."

"Mom," I groan. "I'm trying to concentrate."

"Right," she says softly. There's the gentle sound of the plate being set down on my desk, followed by the quiet click of the door.

I fish out my phone. I dismiss another handful

of notifications and start scrolling through my selfies. Maybe if I find the right angle, the right lighting, Clover will see it. She'll remember how things were, how things could have been. She'll remember she misses me. She does miss me, doesn't she?

Before I can upload the picture, I spot a new post on my feed — Clover's first upload in more than two weeks. My heart skips a beat. It's a picture of a sunset. No caption or tags, just some nature emojis. But I recognize the view. It's from the top of a play structure in a park not that far from here. I give my face one more strong wipe and throw on my jacket.

My sneakers touch the edge of the brown, wet grass. I see her, an outline against a golden sky. A cold breeze hits and I pull my coat closed. She hardly seems to notice me.

"Hey," I call. "What're you doing here?"

She doesn't turn, just stares down at the phone in her hands.

I start climbing. The bars of the jungle gym are cold and slick. I didn't think to bring gloves. But I keep going. I'm nearly halfway up the structure when she finally speaks.

"I'm transgender."

"What?" The wind whistles in my ears. I didn't think to bring a hat either.

"I started transitioning about a year ago," she speaks up and pockets her phone. "It was the best thing I've ever done for myself but . . . my teachers didn't get it. Neither did my parents."

"Clover . . ." My voice shakes as I fight back the damp cold. "I didn't know."

"I wanted a fresh start," she sighs into her hands. "That's all. No distractions, no drama. Somewhere I could just be, you know?" Her laugh is a thin cloud. "And then one night, one stupid night."

"About the video . . ." I try to explain but the words won't form. If only I'd come here as Ren instead.

He'd be so much better at this than I am.

She lifts her face toward me. "This is *so* not about that stupid video."

"It's not?"

A gust of wind smacks against my back. I lose my grip and start to slide. Before I can even gasp, Clover's arm juts out and links with mine.

She pulls me close. Her lips are a breath away. She leans in and closes her eyes. Despite everything inside of me screaming to kiss her, I move away.

Her dark eyes open, looking like polished garnet in the slivers of remaining sunlight. "What?" she whispers. "You don't want to kiss me unless there's a camera in our face?"

The air in my lungs feels like it's turned to stone. "What did you say?"

"On the weekends, online." Clover searches my face, her eyes welling up. "You act like I'm some different person."

My heart jumps into my throat while my stomach drops into my shoes. "You know that I'm . . ."

"Of course I know!" Her laugh is wet and heavy, like someone trying to come up for air. "Lauri, Ren, whatever you want to call yourself, it doesn't matter to me. I *like* you. Don't you like me back?"

I blink as my eyes tear up in the chilly air. The sun is getting low. "I don't know what you're talking about." Even as I say it, I choke on my own lie.

"Oh, my god!" Clover shakes her head and pushes me away. "Can you just stop gaslighting me for, like, two seconds?!" Her lips start to shake. "Was any of this even real to you?"

I don't know what to say. Eventually, my silence is its own answer.

"Well, I've got news for you." She starts to clamber down from her perch. "I'm not your manic-pixie-dream-girl. You don't get to keep using me to make yourself feel better and then throw me away when you get bored." She lands softly and brushes herself off before starting to walk.

"Clover . . ." I find my voice and try to follow her but can barely keep my balance.

"Just leave me alone," she tells me. Soon, she's nothing more than a long shadow vanishing into the early night.

15 Fool's Paradise

THE THICK AIR of the Barn wraps around me like a warm hug. It's the one place where I really feel like I'm home. Maybe I'll chat with Joni, or plan some solo choreo. Anything to get my mind off Clover.

It's only a little after eight but I can already hear music playing. Passing the handful of regulars hanging by the bar, I swing toward the stage. For some reason, Earl's here, running through a set. I didn't get word that we were doing rehearsals today.

"Five, six, seven, eight!" Stormé snaps along. "Nice, good turn, now hold!"

The song fades. Earl hangs for a few seconds in their last pose. Their tawny cheeks glow crimson, the foundation along their brow clumped with sweat. "How was that?" Earl pants. Stormé flashes a bright pink smile. Tara gives a thumbs up from the booth.

There's a loud huff. I spot one of the Olivers sitting by the bar, arms crossed, glaring at the stage. Stormé rolls her eyes as she tosses Earl their water bottle. "The set's looking tight," she says. "Let's run it again, just to be sure."

The short Oliver by the bar clicks his tongue. "But where's the *edge?*" he sighs loudly, stroking his goatee.

"Oliver's got a point." The taller Oliver steps onto the stage and smacks Earl on the shoulder. "The little space gimmick is cute, but isn't it a little . . . overdone?"

"What's going on?" I step from the shadows. Earl's face quickly drains. Stormé hardly glances my way.

"We're hosting a pageant for Pride!" says the taller Oliver. He claps Earl's shoulder again and nearly sends them tumbling.

"First week of June. Relying on these two getting a decent set together," the shorter Oliver scoffs. He sips from a martini glass and raises a fluffy white eyebrow at me. "Here to audition?"

"You're planning another pageant?" My face starts to warm. My nose feels like it's been given a hard pinch.

"We didn't . . ." Earl starts to explain as they duck from Oliver's grip.

Stormé runs shimmering nails through her short pink wig. "Let's go from the top!" She waves toward Tara, who snaps a bubble in response and restarts the track.

"This guy runs you too hard, you know." The taller Oliver nods toward Stormé. "Let the kid rest. He's run the thing into the ground anyway."

"Earl's not a 'he,'" Stormé's voice is calm, but firm.

"And she's, uh, not a guy," Earl stutters in agreement.

The short Oliver groans. "You know what he means!"

"Oliver, Oliver!" Joni practically leaps over the bar. "Can I get your help back here? Both of you?"

Stormé mutters under her breath as the bar owners are led away, Joni giving the rest of us a sorry look.

"You weren't even going to tell me?" I don't bother whispering. If the Olivers and Joni want to listen in on our drama, they're welcome to it.

Stormé turns back toward the stage. "Ren, this is not the time."

"When is the time, then?" I stomp after her. "Because I thought we were supposed to be a *family*." Stormé doesn't flinch. "So, what, I'm just ghosted for no reason?"

"It's not for no reason," Earl steps in.

"You admit it!" I let out a bitter laugh. "What, because I won? You got jealous, thought you'd cut me out of the competition?"

Stormé shakes her head. "You know that's not why."

"Because I messed up with that whole scheduling thing?" I try to swallow the cracking in my voice. "Like you all don't mess up all the time. But one tiny mistake, and I'm cancelled?"

"It wasn't just once, Ren," says an unfamiliar voice. The music cuts off. Above, Tara leans into the mic. "And it wasn't tiny."

I stare up in shock. "I don't think I've ever heard you say that much at once," I admit at last.

"Yeah, because I don't talk to toxic people." Tara takes out a huge wad of gum and places it on the underside of the DJ booth. "But these two aren't going to say it, so I will. Your whole ego-heavy fuckboi thing is not cute. On stage, and especially off. Do you ever think about anybody besides yourself? At all?"

"I don't . . ." I spin to the others. A hoarse laugh escapes from my chest. "Did Tara seriously just call me toxic?"

Stormé watches me sideways. "You're really surprised, after that stunt you tried to pull?"

I stammer, "I was just trying to —"

"Trying to assault a paying customer?" she cuts me off. "Get us all kicked out? Undermine the whole show?"

"That's the only reason you 'won' last time," Tara adds.

My mouth hangs open. "Look, you don't understand everything going on . . ."

"I don't think you understand." Stormé calmly steps toward me. "We've put a lot of work into this showcase. We're trying to make something special, a space that's safer. You violated all of that."

I look around in shock until my eyes land on Earl. "Come on." I lean toward them. "You've got to have my back here."

Earl chews at their cheeks, smearing their glimmering lipstick. "I thought maybe you just needed somebody to be a friend. Show you the ropes, you know?" They let out a slow sigh. "Now, I think . . . I think a real friend is someone who's honest with you. Ren, I can't make excuses for you anymore."

The last words hit me in the chest. "Fine," I murmur, a hitch in my breath. "Forget it. Good luck getting folks for your next show without my name on the set list." Even as I say it, I remember the ethereal dancer from the last pageant. I know in my gut there are plenty of performers who can take my place.

I spin on my heel and almost walk right into the tall Oliver's chest. He looks down his round nose at me. "I'm sorry, who are you again?"

The shorter one appears from behind the bar. "Hey, wait, aren't you that kid that took the crown last time? You're not going for the title again?"

I shake my head. "See you never."

"That's a shame." The taller Oliver steps back towards his partner. "The in-house talent is getting a little sparse."

"We'll double our outreach," Stormé says as she walks swiftly toward them. "Not to mention, I've got a set I've been rehearsing."

"Sure, queen," the shorter Oliver chuckles.

"Are you sure that's quite fair?" says the other as he

looks Stormé up and down. "Don't you think you've . . . got an unfair advantage?"

"Excuse me?!" I hear Tara stomping down from the DJ booth. But the door swings shut behind me, muting the rest of their voices.

I linger around the Barn's front entrance and take in the stillness of Church Street on a Sunday. Normally, I'd find the quiet peaceful. Tonight it's just eerie. Nobody wants to be out in this weather. It's been a long, cold spring and it's starting to feel like summer's never going to get here. Everything will just be damp, gross and awful, forever.

I spot Joni hanging in a nearby alleyway. Puffs of vapour rise into the air. I meander closer and lean against the opposite wall. I give a nod and, when it's met with a chilly silence, I let out a long sigh. "I don't know if you heard what was going on back in there . . ."

"Stop." Joni inhales deeply on a vape. "I don't do the whole therapist-bartender thing when I'm working. And definitely not on my smoke break."

"Oh." I shove my chilly fingers into my pockets. There's another long pause. "But, I was wondering if maybe you could talk to —"

Eyes shut, Joni lets out a cotton cloud. "Nope. Sorry, not sorry. Working at this place, you gotta have boundaries or you just end up messed in every gay's drama."

"Right." The cold rush of air running past us bites my ears.

Joni brushes by me but hovers for a moment longer. "For what it's worth," says the non-therapist bartender. "You do a good show. Just save the act for the stage."

16 *Of You Ever*

AFTER NO CONTACT from my drag family and no new messages from Clover, I'm getting wound up. Last week I got so bored, I ended up hanging out with Mom and Nathan! I had to teach them how to Chromecast and then they made me watch old-people movies from, like, the '90s. Total nightmare.

At the same time, I can go only so long being my own company. Even my internal monologue has started to sound like white noise. It's like I'm fading into the background of my own life.

Turns out, being invisible can have its downsides. For one thing, even if people don't mean to be mean, they can kind of forget about you. Like, when I was getting really desperate, I tried making plans with Devon, Sara and Morgan. They all said they would text me to "get together sometime." Today, I found out they've all gone to the island for Senior Skip Day. Two-thirds of my grade is there. Nobody thought to text me.

As I sit alone in an almost empty cafeteria, it hits me. After graduation, nobody here is going to remember my name. I don't know if they even remember it now.

"Hey, stranger." Rodger sets his lunch bag next to me. The tightness in my chest is suddenly lifted. I start going on about anything and everything I can think of. It's like I'm finally coming up for air. At last, I can talk to someone who might actually listen. Someone else who wasn't cool enough to have been invited to Skip Day, or so I thought.

"Oh, the island thing?" Rodger uses a small cloth to wipe the wax off his apple before taking a bite.

"Yeah, Steph told me about it. Had to miss though. Too much work to get done here."

"Steph, like, Stephanie?" I pop open a bag of chips from the vending machine. They only had Sour Cream and Onion, ugh, the worst. "Since when do you hang with her?"

"Since she ran for finance officer of student government," Rodger tells me like it's no big deal. "She's actually really down to earth, once you get to know her."

"Sure she is," I scoff as I wipe oniony crumbs into my shirt.

"See for yourself." He nibbles on the edges of the apple core. "Swing by our next meeting for prom committee."

"Stephanie's on the committee?" I can't help but laugh at the idea. "What, did Brian sign up too?"

"Yeah, actually." Rodger leans back. He tosses the last of his apple toward the garbage bins and misses by a metre. "Though, I heard he and Steph are on the rocks again."

"It's up to you." Rodger slides up from the table bench and snags the nibbled core from the floor along with a few other pieces of garbage. Sorting his finds into the compost and recycling, he adds, "But you'd really rather spend your lunches eating alone at the trash table?"

I scrunch up my nose. "I don't know, Rod."

"Just trust me on this one." Rodger flashes a silvery smile. A big piece of apple skin pokes from between his braces. "You might be surprised who you see."

As I down the final crumbs of my chip-based lunch, I can't help but think Rodger may have a point. Maybe it's not too late to find people to notice I exist at this school. Besides, it's not like I have anything else to do.

It sounded fine in theory. I was just going to pop in and see what this whole committee thing was about. Then I could bounce if they tried to get me to actually volunteer for anything. Now I'm here, facing down a door with a taped paper sign that reads: *Prom Committee: Meeting in Progress.* There are hearts and stars doodled in the corners that look to be Stephanie's handiwork.

I'm ready to turn right back around when the door swings open. The surprised face of Stephanie herself stares back at me. Behind her, others try to get a peek at who is interrupting their meeting.

"You're not Rodger," says Stephanie.

"You sure?" I give a sideways smile.

"Lauri, glad you could make it!" A hand claps my shoulder. Rodger flashes a grin and slides past me. "Hey, Steph," he says.

Steph's face bursts into a smile. She twirls a ringlet of her hair and steps quickly alongside Rodger. "We've been wondering where you were, silly!"

The pair are quickly enveloped by the rest of the chattering committee keeners. I recognize a few faces. Some band and theatre kids. A couple nerds who usually skip lunch for chess club. There are even a few of the athletic types who run circles around me in gym. What's really surprising, though, is how well Rodger blends in with all of them. Now that he's here, no one seems to even glance my way.

There's a tight circle of plastic chairs. I pick a spot with an empty seat on either side. Rodger eventually pulls away from his group and comes to sit next to me. I look around at the bustling space and say, "I thought you were struggling to get members."

"We were," Rodger chuckles. "But the musical wrapped. Same with Model UN. And —"

"But how did you *get* them here?" I shake my head at him. "What, are you paying people to sign up?"

"They're my friends," Rodger shrugs.

"You have friends?" I say it before I can think not to. "Uh, I don't mean . . ." I start stammering. "Of course you do . . ."

Rodger laughs, giving me a nudge before pointing out people around the room. "Those three I know from photography club. She's on the debate team. That couple's from the Black Students Alliance. I met Alvin and his friend in the GSA . . ."

"But . . ." I pinch my brows together. My head is starting to hurt. "You're always sitting alone at lunch and stuff."

"Mm, I think *you* were always sitting alone at lunch." Rodger points two finger-guns at me. "I sat *with* you."

I stare blankly at the dorky, weird kid I thought I knew. Eventually, I ask quietly, "We have a GSA?"

"Yeah! Those Spectrum meetings? I tried to bring you, like, five times!" Rodger pokes me in the shoulder and nods toward the corner. "We have a lot of people from there after Mrs. Burchum replaced Mr. Mandelo as our faculty supervisor. She runs both clubs now." Following his eyes, I spot Mrs. B in the corner tackling a book of Sudoku. For the first time, I notice a small rainbow pin on her vest.

"Burchum's a lesbian?" I look around to see if anyone else is shocked. Along the way, I spot Brian sulking at the other end of the circle. He's staring longingly at Stephanie but she doesn't seem to notice. Then there's Kyler, holding hands with one of the stoner guys whose locker is just a few down from mine. "Is Kyler gay too?!"

Rodger shushes me as heads turn our direction. "Where've you been?" He nudges me. "He came out as bi in, like, grade ten!"

"Sorry I'm late!" Clover bursts in to a round of hellos. The second our eyes meet, we both freeze. I thought Rodger said she'd dropped out of the committee!

As if reading my mind, Rodger flashes me a wink.

"Okay, everyone," he says as he waves to circle up the group. "Let's get started!"

17 Gut Feeling

AS THE MEMBERS of the prom committee take their seats, I realize with a sinking feeling that the only open chair is right next to me. Clover reluctantly takes the seat, her face tight. I search myself for something, anything, to say. Just then, my watch loudly beeps.

"All devices on silent, please." Rodger raises his eyebrow toward me. "Now, any points people would like to raise before we read the minutes?"

"Do we really have to read the minutes?" asks the guy holding Kyler's hand. "We all know how last week went down. We argued theme for an hour, and then said we'd decide next week. *Again*."

"Skyler's right," Stephanie pipes up. "Even if we don't all agree, we need to pick something. Maybe a majority vote?"

"Good point, Steph." Rodger nods. He pulls a notebook from his pocket and scribbles something down. Brian snorts loudly and sinks deeper into his chair.

I try to listen, but all I can think about is Clover. Her arm is right next to mine, so close I can feel electricity tingling along my skin. Does she feel it too? I try to sneak a look at her from the corner of my eye. I swear I catch her doing the same.

"I have to disagree," says one of the band geeks. "Consensus decision is one of our collective guidelines. We're supposed to just bypass that because it's difficult?"

"What do you care?" asks a tall kid next to her. "You weren't even here when they made those rules!"

"Fair call," Rodger says as he taps his pen against the notepad. "Maybe we should dedicate today to recrafting the group agreements." A groan ripples through the room.

At my wrist, my watch flickers with another message. Amid the heated debate, I take a peek.

Earl: Hey Ren.

Earl: How you been?

My stomach sinks like a rock. Total silence for weeks, now they're texting me like everything's normal? I would guess it was a wrong number thing, but there's my name right there. Now that Earl has seen my read receipt, they're typing more.

"You can't be serious!" Stephanie rolls her eyes and tosses back her hair. "How is *The Witcher* an appropriate theme for a prom?"

"How is it *not*?" says a kid with rainbow suspenders. "Have you not seen the show? Geralt can *get it*."

"You have to admit, it's better than your idea," chimes in a guy wearing a Supreme T-shirt. "*Winter Wonderland* doesn't even make sense. It's in summer!"

"It's a commentary on climate change!" Stephanie whines. The whole committee breaks out into argument again.

Another notification. This time I don't open it, just check the preview.

Earl: Could we get together and talk? I've been thinking a lot and . . .

"If you're gonna do a stupid movie," Brian grunts, "why not do an actually funny one. Like, *Ace Ventura* or something?"

Before I can think twice, I let out a loud gag. The whole room goes quiet. Brian is staring me down. I guess he's not used to people disagreeing with him. I ball up my hands and feel my palms start to sweat.

"You got beef with Jim Carrey?" Brian snarls.

I can't believe it. He actually looks serious. I'm about to drop it but, when I open my mouth, a snarky voice climbs out of my throat. "What, you fall asleep before the ending?" It's like I'm suddenly Ren again. And I'm in no mood to be stared down by a basic hetero bro who doesn't even know how to regulate his

Axe body spray. "He voms after basically kissing a trans woman. Or is that funny to you?"

There's a smattering of laughter. I even spot Mrs. Burchum look up from her Sudoku with a smirk. Brian's shoulders go up as he mutters something like *snowflake* under his breath.

I know I have only a few seconds to get in a real point. I search the back of my head, trying to find Ren's words again. Instead I remember something Stormé said. "I just don't think that would help make the space feel safer for everyone."

"Yeah, dude, grow up already," Kyler says, punching Brian in the shoulder. "Homophobia is so gay."

"I know that," Brian huffs. He turtles back down. "I was just testing you all."

My wrist lights up again. Another message from Earl. My short-gained confidence quickly falls away. I stand and head for the door.

Rodger glances up from his rapid scribbling. "Lauri, where you going?"

"I just need some air," I say, already halfway out of the room. As I look back, for the first time in what feels like forever, I see Clover give me a quiet smile. There's a fluttering in my chest but I can't hold her gaze. I softly shut the door behind me.

It looks like Earl's sending me a whole book. Exhausted, I flip the chat on do-not-disturb. *I'll read it later*, I tell myself. I just need to clear my head. My stomach grumbles loudly and I start toward the cafeteria. I'm already daydreaming what vending machine meal I can get today.

18 Through Enough

I STARE DOWN AT MY FINAL EXAM. All I hear is the click of Madame Dorit's pacing steps. I tap my pencil in one hand. I know I should know this stuff. I even studied. But it's like somebody tilted me to one side and four years of high-school French just completely fell out of my head.

I sneak a look around the gym, again. Just on the off chance that one of Clover's classes are taking their exam in here too. No such luck. I can almost picture her, crouched over one of the desks they pull in for finals. Her glasses slipping down her nose as she concentrates on multiple-choice questions. I imagine us sipping tea at her Granny's house, studying for our exams. She'd make finals prep a whole lot more fun, though I'd probably just be a distraction to her.

One of the invigilators glares at me from the front of the room. I duck my head and go back to staring blankly at the pages in front of me. I doodle a pair of round spectacles in the corner of my workbook.

After a while, the letters slowly start to come together to form a few words I recognize. There are even a couple sentences in there. I do as much as I can, then answer B for the rest of the multiple-choice ones. Next up, the essay portion. My head starts to feel like it's pulsing, so I stick my hand in the air to ask for a bathroom break. Madame Dorit reluctantly allows it, insisting on following along.

"Where do you think you're going?" Madame Dorit grumbles as I start off down the hall. "The ladies' room is this way."

"Yeah, but the gender-neutral bathroom's back here." I point over my shoulder. That's what they renamed the accessible bathroom last week. Rodger said it was a Spectrum initiative. I wouldn't know. I never did make it to any of those meetings.

Madame Dorit twists up her face so tight, it looks like she's about to pop. Still, she lets me go to the single-stall and takes up a post waiting outside.

Finally alone, I release a long sigh. It feels like I've been holding my breath for ages. I run my hands under the cold water and splash my face a few times before looking around. It's actually kind of nice in here. I wish I had my phone or something. At least the teachers didn't take my smartwatch. I don't think most of them even knew what it was.

There's a buzz at my wrist and I instinctively check it. Not that I'm getting any important messages. Just another stream of pointless notifications. Looks like somebody took a still of my face from that stupid video and turned it into a meme. Somebody has tagged me in a compilation. Great, that's exactly what I need right now.

I try to zone out by scrolling onto Facebook. First thing I see is an update from the prom committee. Looks like they picked a date, first week of June. What really gets me, though, is the picture. There's Rod and the rest of them, all hanging out to paint a banner and craft decorations. I spot Stephanie in the background, flicking paint at Kyler and his boyfriend. Clover's right there with them, laughing away.

I feel like I should be jealous, but I'm happy for her. She's got a group of friends and she can just be herself with them. That's all she really wanted. I think I might have even gone back to committee meetings, but I didn't know if she could relax with me there. She told me to leave her alone, right? After everything, maybe that's really what's best.

Against my better judgement, I go to the event page and start poking around. All I find are posts from the admins. One is asking if anybody knows any musical acts or a DJ for the big night. There's a pang in my gut as I remember that I don't have anyone to suggest — at least, not anymore.

My watch screen goes dark. My own face stares back at me. From this angle, I can see my double chin. That spot where I tried to shave a sliver of my eyebrow and it never really grew back. The scar that rests just under my nose from when I was eight and got dinged by a stray softball. Mom didn't want me going to practice after that. I don't know if the other kids even noticed I was gone. Same old invisible Lauri.

It's my face, but it doesn't feel like it. Someone else is looking through my eyes. He's still in there. I always told myself that Ren was just an idea. Someone I pretended to be on the weekend, to let off steam. Now I'm starting to wonder if he was the realest thing about me. And if that's what I'm really like? Well, maybe everyone is right to keep their distance.

It's really his fault all this happened. Messing things up with Clover, the pageant, my drag family. At the same time, if he never existed, I don't know who I'd even be.

I wouldn't have ever known what it was like to be under that spotlight. To dance like everyone is watching and loving every second of it. I'd never have had the guts to actually talk to a beautiful girl at a streetcar stop. Or go to a thrift store and try on the things I actually want to wear. I don't know if I'd ever have felt like I was really alive, not just moving from day to day. Still, maybe it's time for Ren to learn something from Lauri about the art of going invisible.

An impatient knock at the door breaks my train of thought. "Lauren Garber," Madame Dorit says in her forced French accent. "You are well past *temps* for a *pause de toilette*."

I flush the toilet and turn the sink on full blast. "Almost done!" I holler back.

"*Mademoiselle*, if you think I am going to wait out here for *une* more minute . . ." Madame Dorit starts ranting, which should buy me at least another thirty seconds. "You are risking *l'expulsion* from *l'examination*!"

It's worth it. If I don't do it now, I don't know if I ever will. I haven't posted anything on Ren's account since the video blew up. It's time to break the silence.

I press my smartwatch camera against my leg and

manage to get a picture of a fully black screen. I start to type a post under it. Writing as fast as I can, I put down what I should have said in the first place.

I tell the truth. I tried to kiss the woman in the video without asking first. The whole thing is on me. I outline an apology for the way I was acting, not just on stage, but off too. At the end, I let them know that the performance in the video was my final show. @The.Real.Ren is officially retiring.

19 On Your Mind

"OUCH!" I yelp as Mom struggles to comb through my hair.

"Your hair is so dry," she mutters as she teases my fried-out bangs. "Have you not been conditioning?"

"Whatever." I pull my head back, ducking into my hoodie. "I told you, I'm not going. I feel sick."

"Nonsense." Mom pats me on the shoulder and sets down the brush. "What nice young lady wants to skip her own prom?!"

"I'm *not* a nice young lady," I grumble. She doesn't hear me as she busies herself with the makeup bag on my desk.

"Mascara . . . Foundation . . . Eyeliner . . . Lauri, don't you have anything with a little colour?" She searches deeper for something we both know she's not going to find. "Maybe a little lipstick?"

"I don't need lipstick," I tell her. I yank at the bag.

"Of course, sweetheart." She smiles gently at me. "You're already so beautiful. And I've got just the thing to bring out that perfect smile of yours!" She stands up and practically skips out of the room, to my great, if temporary, relief.

I'm supposed to be relaxing. Finals have come and gone. I managed average grades, as usual. That's Lauri, average. Now high school is finally over. I know I'll be the first one everyone forgets. All the signatures in my yearbook had messages like: *Good luck with everything*, or, worse, *Have a great summer!* Who even says that?

My watch lights up on my desk. I told myself I

wouldn't check it but I can't help myself. It's a reminder for an event I "might be interested in," the second official All-Ages Drag Pageant at the Barn. I've been following the official Insta page for a couple weeks, under @LaurenGarborator, of course. I don't want them to know how invested I am. It's weird but, honestly, I care way more about the pageant now than I did when I was a part of the first one.

It seems like everything has gone deluxe. There's a new stage installed and some seriously big-name performers. They even got a DJ who played in Montreal last year. The whole thing is supposed to pop off in a couple of hours. How about that — prom and the pageant on the same night. And here I am, not going to either. Sounds about right.

My sulking is interrupted by another notification. Somebody asked a question on the pageant's newest post. **@ChimpmunkChad asks:** Will @The.Real.Ren be there?

Underneath, they put a gif of my face pasted onto some guy falling into a dunk tank. Real nice. Must have taken time to do that one.

I toss my watch onto the bed, next to my silenced phone. Nobody I actually want to talk to is going to be messaging me, even if they wanted to. I muted the WhatsApp chat with Stormé, Earl and Tara. Blocked them all on Snap, too. I know it's petty. But every time I saw their names it made my stomach twist into knots. Meanwhile, the only person I haven't blocked still hasn't said a word, online or IRL. I can't really blame her. I wouldn't want to talk to me either. There's nothing I can say at this point to really change things. I need to let them all move on, and figure out how to do the same.

I slip a collared shirt from my closet around my shoulders. Pull on a pair of pants that squeeze a little but make my butt look just right. When I look in the mirror, I see a glimpse of the person I've been looking for. There's a knot in my stomach as I realize that my days of being Ren are behind me.

I never thought my time in drag would be over so quickly. I miss the glare of the lights, the way the music pulsed through my whole body and made me come alive. Even more, I miss the people. Not the fans. My friends. My family. I could do drag again, go find some other scene. Maybe move to another city and start all over again. But I don't think I'd ever find something like what we had together.

"Here it is!" Mom twirls back into my room. Glowing with pride, she holds out a shimmering gown. "Surprise!"

"Oh, Mom." My chest goes tight. "You . . . shouldn't have."

"I know, it's a little retro," she sighs. She runs her hand along the glittering fabric. "But I think your measurements aren't that far from mine when I was your age."

"It's yours?" I ask, inching backward.

"Don't worry, I got it dry-cleaned." She winks at me. Then her eyes wander down. "Oh." Her smile dips, only slightly. "Is that what you'd like to wear tonight?"

"What, this?" I force a laugh and start to untuck my shirt. "No! I was just, uh, finding some stuff for donation! You know, I've always got too many clothes in my closet."

She gently sets the dress at the edge of my bed. Her face softens. For the first time, I notice the small wrinkles around the edges of her eyes. "Nathan and I will be downstairs whenever you're ready for pictures," she says. Before she leaves, she pauses. "Kiddo, is there anything you want to tell me?"

There's a knock on my door.

"Lauri, um," Nathan appears, awkward as ever. "Someone's here to see you." My heart leaps into my throat. It has to be Clover. She came to ask me to prom after all! "Should I tell him to wait in the living room?"

"Him?" I say out loud. I feel my mom's eyes drilling into me.

"He said his name was Rodger," Nathan answers.

Mom takes her sweet time lingering in the hall. Meanwhile, here's Rodger, all done up in his sharp suit and a fresh fade. Even got his braces off. He's actually kind of . . . not totally terrible. He fiddles with his boutonniere and says, "I came to see if you wanted to go to prom."

A laugh bursts through me so hard I double over. I prop myself up on my chair. For some reason, his serious face makes me laugh even harder. "You?" I gasp, feeling a cramp pinching at my side. "You want to go to prom . . . with me?!"

"Obviously not," he huffs. "I've already got a date, thank-you-very-much."

I look at him sideways and start to regain my breath. "Someone owe you a favour for helping with their homework?" As soon as I say it, I wish I could take it back. So I do. "Sorry, that was mean."

Rodger steps over to my window. The sky is orange with streetlamps and city light. He speaks softly. "I've been worried about you."

"Me? Why would you be worried about me?" I grab the dress off my bed and shake its sparkly layers. "I was getting ready to go."

"I'm on committee, Lauri. I know you didn't get a ticket."

We both go quiet. I can hear my mother and Nathan shuffling downstairs. "I didn't mean to not get one," I admit. "I just sort of forgot. Besides, it's for the best. Prom's stupid anyway."

"You're stupid!" Rodger spins. He looks like I just punched him in the gut. "Do you listen to yourself? What, you think you're 'not like other girls' because you can't be bothered to give a crap?"

"I mean, I'm really not like other girls . . ." I say out of the side of my mouth.

"Don't you think I know that?" Rodger starts to pace. "We've been neighbours for the last fifteen years. You don't think I see you sneaking out, coming home late?"

I blink at him. "You live around here?"

"I'm, like, four houses down." Rodger furrows his brow. "Lauri, do you pay attention to anyone else but yourself? Look, I know something's been going on with you. I don't totally get it but cutting yourself off from everyone isn't going to help."

He reaches into his coat pocket and unfolds a small

paper. "I brought you this, in case you change your mind." He lets it drop onto the bed before turning to leave. It's a prom ticket.

Nathan appears at my bedroom door again, blocking Rodger's mic-drop exit. "Um, Lauri?" he says, "I think more of your friends are here." Rodger and I share a look. Who else do I even know? "I think they're from your youth group."

20 Grateful

I MUST BE HALLUCINATING. That's the only explanation. I've lost it or fallen into a coma. Maybe I died and this is what my hell looks like. Because I know there's no way my whole ex-drag-family is sitting around my kitchen table.

Nathan fetches a ginger ale for Earl. Stormé and Tara are making small talk with my mom. "So, where did you say it's hosted?" Mom asks.

"Church," Tara answers. Stormé flashes me a wink

as I step downstairs.

Mom touches her cheek and glances in my direction. "Honey, you never said it was a *religious* group."

"What are you doing?!" I gape. I nearly trip on the last step.

Mom gives a stern look. "I'm welcoming our guests, Lauri."

"Yeah, Lauri," Tara snickers until Stormé shoots over a glare, looking almost like my mother for a second.

"Donna," Stormé taps lightly on my mother's hand. "Would you give us a minute?"

To my shock, Mom gives her a pleasant smile and steps aside. "It's nice to finally meet your friends, dear," she tells me quietly. "Such nice young people. A little eccentric maybe . . . Does that short one have on pointy ears?"

Nathan steps back in the room, proudly presenting a ginger ale complete with bendy straw. I press him and Mom toward the living room. Once I'm sure they're out of earshot, I spin around to the group and ask, "What the hell's going on?!"

"Well, you were avoiding us online," says Earl, happily sipping their pop. "We figured we'd have to come get you IRL."

I search their faces. "Me, avoiding you?"

"Did you just say 'IRL' in real life?" Rodger asks over my shoulder. The whole room, even me, turns to him in one motion. I kind of forgot he was still here. "Sorry!" he says quickly and backs up against the counter.

"Who's the sidepiece?" Tara raises an eyebrow, loudly chewing on a fresh wad of pink gum.

"Never mind him," I shrug. "How did you even find me?"

"You're not as stealth as you think you are," laughs Stormé. She throws a rainbow braid behind her shoulder. "What matters is that we're here, we're queer and we're taking you with us."

"But . . ." I blink down at the floor. "Why?"

"The Olivers have been up our butts trying to

run the whole pageant!" Earl smacks down their drink, nearly spilling it over the table. "Most of the acts they picked are *way* old! Like, what's even the point of an all-ages show?"

"They even booked some out-of-towner to DJ," Tara says through a scowling bubble-gum pop. "I don't think he's even queer."

"But how am I supposed to help with all that?" I glance back to make sure Mom and Nathan aren't listening in.

"We need someone who knows how the show used to be." Stormé steeples her fingers. "Someone who's not afraid to be . . . pushy."

"We need an asshole," says Tara, slipping in another stick of gum.

"So this is just about tonight." My eyes start to sting. I hear Stormé say something about how it's not like that, but I mutter, "No, it's okay, I get it. I messed up."

There's a touch at my arm. "We saw your post online," says Earl, giving it a gentle pat. "About retiring."

"Yeah." My shoulders slump. "I'm sorry about . . . you

know, everything. It's probably best if I just hang back for now."

I pull away but Tara blocks my exit. "As if. You're not getting off that easy."

Earl holds me in place. "Stop running away," they tell me. "Help us fix it."

"You're still a part of our family, Ren." Stormé stands and puts her hand on my shoulder. "If you want to be."

I open my mouth to speak but nothing comes out. This is all I wanted, but I can't seem to believe it's real.

"What about tonight though?" Rodger asks, leaning against the countertop.

"For real, who is this guy?" Tara gives him a sidelong glance. "You doing drag with him now?"

"Sort of," I smirk. "The thing is, tonight, it's sort of . . . prom?"

"Seriously?!" Earl squeals and clutches their hands together. "Is this your date?"

"No!" Rodger and I say at once.

"He just came to check up on me," I try to explain.

"I *was* going to ask someone but . . . I don't think she's into me anymore."

"Who, Clover?" Rodger says. "I wouldn't count her out just yet." My jaw drops, but he just flashes a toothy grin. "Your friends are right. You really aren't as sneaky as you think."

"What are we waiting for, then?" Earl gives me a playful shove. "Let's get you to prom!"

Stormé looks me over and nods. "We can salvage this. I've got some supplies in the car."

"But what about the pageant? Aren't you going to be late?" I ask.

"Let the Olivers have it." Tara pops another big bubble. "This sounds like more fun than watching some rando mixing in *my* booth anyway."

I push up my bangs and let myself break out into a smile. "Rod, do you think you could maybe swing a plus-three onto that ticket you got for me?"

"I think I have another idea . . ." Rodger mutters as he and the others head out.

I'm almost to the door when Mom catches me.

"Lauri, sweetheart, are you leaving?"

"Yeah," I say, hardly glancing back. "My friends and I are going to prom!"

"That's great!" She claps. "Let's get a picture!"

I groan, but Stormé pops her head in. "Did someone say picture?"

Next thing I know, I'm sandwiched between Stormé and Earl, while Tara pulls a face that makes Rodger bust a gut. "One more!" says Mom from behind her tablet as she snaps another dozen photos.

"Mom . . ." I whine.

Nathan comes traipsing from upstairs with something in his fist. "H-here," he tells me. He loops a red tie around my neck and quickly knots it under my collar. "My good luck charm."

"Now, isn't that handsome." Mom steps back to get a good look before taking another shot.

And honestly? I'm grateful.

21 I'm Coming Out

"ARE YOU SURE I'll be able to get in?" I ask as I pencil in a thin beard using Stormé's spare eyeliner. "I don't exactly look like my student ID right now."

"Don't worry about that." Rodger leans over to look out the side window. "I'll explain everything when we get to the door."

"About that," says Tara from the driver's seat. "We might have a little trouble."

Rodger said they booked some old hotel for

the prom. As we pull up, I peer over and spot a huge crowd at the venue's entrance. The mass of people only vaguely holds the shape of an actual line. There are queens with towering updos, twinks in platform heels and mesh, a couple leather bears — well, cubs — and more. They're sporting rainbow flags on nearly every place you'd ever imagine a flag could go. Mixed in are a handful of straight-laced students and parents looking mortified.

"Whoops," Earl says and sinks back in their seat.

I blink at them in shock. "What did you do?!"

"Maybe just one little post." They fiddle with the shiny pink pop-socket on their phone. "Telling folks we were doing a venue change."

Stormé raises her already arched brows. "You told them the pageant was relocating?"

"Oh, no!" Earl answers. "I said where *we* were gonna be." They show us a selfie with the rest of us in the background, getting ready in the car. They've tagged Stormé, Tara and @The.Real.Ren. I spot about a hundred likes and comments underneath.

As we park, the commotion by the front door heats up. A woman with short blonde hair shouts something about her son's "special day." Meanwhile, a handful in the rainbow crowd take their chance to slip inside.

Rodger hops out and motions for us to follow his lead. "There's another entrance, around back." He takes us to a plain grey door that leads into a dark hallway. Cramped by stacks of spare chairs and upturned tables, he navigates us through the shadows.

We stop just short of a heavy red curtain. On the other side, I catch drifting fragments of conversation, shuffling feet and last year's pop hits. "All right, this should work," Rodger whispers, nodding to Tara. "You're the DJ, right? The booth's up that way and —"

"Got it." Tara gives a peace sign, already strutting off toward a set of winding stairs. "Later, cutie."

Rodger gives a flustered wave as Tara disappears. He straightens his jacket and motions at a handful of speakers and sound equipment. He grabs a wireless microphone. "Okay, I'll go out there and explain we got some last-minute talent —"

"I can take care of that," says Stormé, plucking the mic out of his hand. "Ren, you ready to go on?"

I've been waiting for those words more than anything else. Everything in me wants to scream, "*Yes, yes, let me back in that spotlight!*" But something in the back of my head gives me pause.

"Actually, I've been thinking." I rub at my chin, then look down and see a smear across my fingers. I've probably just smudged off half my beard. I shake my head — there's not much to do about it now. I put my cleaner hand on Earl's shoulder. "I know you've been working really hard for this, Earl. Why don't you go first?"

"You mean it?" Earl's eyes light up and they squeal so loud they could pop a speaker. They wrap themselves around me in a hug. "I knew you had a heart!"

It's sort of a sad compliment, but I take it anyway.

"All right, all right," Stormé says, pulling Earl off me. "Ren, you'll be second then . . ."

"No." I shake my head. "The thing is, the crowd that showed up? They're probably here because of that stupid video. Which means, after they see me, they might just ditch. Which isn't fair." I shrug toward the curtain. "You should go up before me. I'll close us out."

Stormé tilts her head. "Well, I have been working on something," she admits. She gives me a pat on my cheek and says, "You know, I'm only nineteen and I already feel like I've been at this drag-mother thing way too long."

As the others get in position, Rodger looks around one last time before backing toward the curtain. "See you later then," he says with a wave.

"Wait, where are you going?" I follow him around the drape's edge. On the other side, I find a sparkling room, decorated with a mish-mash of colour palettes. It's actually kind of nauseating trying to take it all in. But if I don't focus on any one thing, it kind of works together.

A table of at least half a dozen members of the prom committee stand around in ties and flowing gowns. One of them calls out to Rodger in a sing-song voice. It's Stephanie, wearing a sash that reads *Valedictorian*.

"It looks like you've all got it handled back there," Rodger says to me. He smiles back at Steph. "I can't leave my date waiting."

"You're here with . . ." I watch in shock as Rodger hurries off to Stephanie's side. The pair are whipped into a conversation with the rest of the group. I recognize a few faces. There's even Mrs. B herself with her arm around a short woman, the two of them rocking matching burgundy pantsuits.

In the middle of them all, there's Clover. She's wearing the most stunning dress, glowing like the sun. Before I can hide again, she turns and catches my gaze. She blinks at me from behind her large, round frames.

22 Loved By You

THE DOORS TO THE HALL BURST OPEN, letting in a flood of rainbow-themed party-crashers followed by a handful of scrambling security guards. The crowd starts to scatter and the lights drop into darkness. A new playlist kicks on, one with a lot more bass. Seems like Tara has made it to the booth. Earl comes out with the mic and tries to work the crowd.

Clover steps quietly to my side. We watch the show unfold. "I didn't know you were coming," she says. Just hearing her voice makes my whole body shiver.

"Me neither," I admit. Taking my chance, I tell her, "Hey, I'm really sorry about pulling that stunt with you at the bar. It wasn't cool. At all."

"And?" She's still studying the room.

Despite the crowd's confusion, they seem to be coming around. Earl goes into their set.

"And I'm sorry for lying to you," I go on. My fingers accidentally brush across hers. A light shock runs up my arm. "Pretending like I was somebody else, acting like you weren't smart enough to figure stuff out."

"And?" she asks again.

My heart feels like it's sinking into my stomach. Meanwhile my stomach feels like it's going to slip into my shoes. "And I totally get if you never want to talk to me again."

She doesn't answer. The two of us watch as Earl twirls through their number. It's the most shimmering, fantastic, over-the-top bit I've seen from them yet. As they finish, they let loose two handfuls of glitter into the audience. The front row ducks back but can't avoid the sparkling clouds. The rest of the room unleashes a wave of applause.

Rodger quickly comes on the mic. He brushes off his suit jacket as he thanks the room for joining us in a surprise, early celebration of Pride Month. People seem to buy it, classmates and chaperones clap along. Up next, Stormé gets ready to belt out a ballad.

Clover turns and holds out her hand. "Do you want to dance?"

My palms instantly feel damp. I swallow my anxiety and take her in my arms. We join a handful of others who've turned the front row into a dance floor. As the two of us step in close circles, I worry my hands are going to leave sweat stains on her dress.

"Now, don't get any ideas," she says in what I hope is a joking tone. "My parents are right over there."

"What? Where?!" I gasp. "Do you need me to get them to leave?"

Clover tilts her head. I follow her gaze to an awkward-looking couple hanging nervously near the snack table. Clover is the spitting image of her mom, but she is tall like her dad. They look a lot less . . . evil than I imagined. Granny hunches over next to them, cramming crudités into her mouth.

"I thought you didn't get along?" I ask.

Clover purses her lips. "You and me?"

"You and your parents," I say. "With the whole trans thing? I thought they kicked you out. Made you live at your Gran's."

Clover's glasses slip down her nose. "No, that stuff's way sorted. My parents are chill with my transition. I moved in with Granny so I could get into a different school district." She spins me around, taking the lead. "Plus, my folks have been super stressed about me applying to uni out of province, so I wanted to show them I could be more independent."

"Wow, okay." I feel my face get rosy. I try to focus on my footing. It's hard enough to dance forward, let alone go backward!

"I thought I wanted to start over. Go somewhere

without so many distractions." She leans in to whisper into my ear. "And then, I met you."

"Right," I mutter to my shoes. "Sorry, again."

A soft touch runs along my chin. Clover lifts my face to hers. "I didn't say it was a bad thing." She brushes a soft kiss against my lips. My breath catches in my throat as I trip over my own feet. She lets out a gentle laugh into my mouth.

Stormé wraps up her performance, leaving hardly a dry eye in the house. She takes to the mic grinning. "Thank you, thank you so much!" As much as I never want to pull away from Clover, I see Stormé beckoning me over. "Now, last but not least . . ."

Clover lifts her arms from my shoulders. "I'll see you when you get back."

"Coming out of *Ren*tirement . . ." Stormé continues. The stirring excitement around the room buys me another second of time.

"Wait," I reach back toward Clover. "Will you go to prom with me?"

Clover giggles and squeezes my hand. "Yes! Now, go!"

Stormé welcomes me into the spotlight. The room erupts in some cheers, a handful of boos. A bunch pull out their phones to start filming. I hear someone whisper that they think they recognize me. Whether they mean from the memes or from school, it's impossible to say. It doesn't matter anymore. I hang there, feeling the lights beating down on me.

I'm here. This is real. I am real. I take a deep breath and let the music fill me up. It's my song.

Acknowledgements

I'd like to thank Bill and Cheryl. You took me in, drove me to school on weekdays and to drag shows on weekends. Best taxi service anyone's ever had. Tony and Heather, you've always had a seat for me at your table, no matter how I arrived. Your steadfast love means more than words can say.

My friends in Winnipeg, for being there during the best and worst times of my young life.

My editor, Kat Mototsune, for believing in my vision. Myriad Augustine, for the editorial (and emotional) guidance. Caitlin Chee, for helping ensure this story's accuracy to burlesque and drag communities in Toronto. Hannah Dees, for making sure this book doesn't sound too out of touch.

Andrew McAllister, for loving me with your whole heart. All my dear friends and chosen family, for supporting my writing process and times it was a not-writing process.

Perhaps most of all, to the reader of this book. You make this all possible.